# The Yeah, Baby Series

## FIONA DAVENPORT

# Copyright

© 2016 Fiona Davenport
All rights reserved.
Edited by PREMA Romance Editing.

All rights reserved. No part of this book may be reproduced or transmitted in any form or by any means, electronic or mechanical, including photocopying, recording, or by any information storage and retrieval system, without permission in writing. For permission requests, please send your email request to authorfionadavenport@yahoo.com.

This is a work of fiction. Names, characters, places and incidents are the product of the author's imagination or are used factiously, and any resemblance to any actual persons or living or dead, events or locales are entirely coincidental.

The author acknowledges the trademark status and trademark owners of various products referenced in this work of fiction, which have been used without permission. The publication/ Use of these trademarks is not authorized, associated with, or sponsored by the trademark owner.

*The pregnancy might be accidental, but their love is not.*

# Baby, You're Mine

Yeah, Baby 1

## FIONA DAVENPORT

## Chapter 1

## WYATT

I stepped inside the dark and smoky interior of Jumpin' Jacks, the only bar in Red Springs, Nebraska. It wasn't far out of North Platte, but it was the nearest place to hang out without going into the city. I squinted as my eyes adjusted and scanned the room, but didn't see the friend I was supposed to meet. Winding my way through the tables, I approached the bar and caught the eye of Wendy, the bartender. I lifted my chin in greeting, and she smiled, winking one heavily kohl-lined eye before grabbing a beer, popping the top, and sliding it down to my waiting hand.

Wendy's smile widened and she flipped her bleached blonde hair over one bony shoulder. She swept her eyes over my body before she turned to help the next customer. My best friend and I had been coming to this bar since we were of legal age. Wendy hadn't stopped trying to get into my pants since she poured me my first drink. After years of ignoring the fake boobs in my face and other not-so-subtle hints, you'd think she would get a clue. And yet, there I was, practically being violated by her direct and clearly dirty stare. Not that I had a problem with any woman picturing me naked and dreaming of doing filthy things to me, but I did have some standards.

"Neat trick."

I froze with my beer halfway to my mouth. The soft, sultry voice washed over me, leaving me with a tightening in my pants and a racing heart. *Yes, from just a fucking voice.* However, my cock came to full attention when I got a look at the owner of the sexy voice. Long, glossy red curls, large, round, bright blue eyes, high cheekbones, and the most kissable lips I had ever seen in my life. But, what had my mouth watering were her curves. She had an hourglass figure that would give Marilyn Monroe a run for her money. Her tits would spill out of my hands, her hips were perfect to hold while I pounded into her from behind, and she was tall—her legs a mile long and showing off a good amount of skin from her short skirt riding up as she sat on a stool. I had a sudden urge to either tug it down as far as it would go or throw a jacket over them. Nobody should see those creamy, white thighs, but me. I finally realized I was standing there gaping, ok leering, at her and pried my jaw up from the ground.

I put on my best panty-melting smile, making sure my dimples popped. "Trick?" I asked.

She smiled and gestured toward the bar. "The thing where you caught the bottle. If I tried the same thing, it would mostly likely end up in my lap, or crashing into the person behind me." She laughed and holy fuck, the rich, genuine sound was the last straw, the one that tipped over the mountain of hay.

*I fell.*

"Wyatt Kincaid," I informed her, holding out my hand. She took it and started to shake, but I brought it to my lips and brushed a kiss across the back. She blushed, and my heart started pounding, desire coursing through my veins.

"Bailey Cross."

"Are you new in town?" I asked, taking a seat on the empty stool next to her.

She took a sip of her martini and her eyes darted away. "Sort of." When her gaze returned to mine, a blush had stolen across her cheeks and she shifted in her chair, suddenly nervous. "I just finished my first year teaching and I'm out for the summer. So, I came here to..." she trailed off and swallowed.

"I'm spending time with family." She gulped down the rest of her martini and pushed the glass away.

"Another?" I asked, and when she nodded, I signaled to the other bartender, Brad, grateful Wendy was busy. I excused myself for a minute to pull out my phone and send a text to my best friend.

**Me:** *You're late, asshole. Find yourself another wingman tonight.*

**Jack:** *Is that code for you found pussy to chase instead of my finely sculpted ass?*

**Me:** *Sure. If that makes you feel better.*

**Jack:** *Breaking bro code, dude.*

**Me:** *Bro code is null and void if there is a chance to get laid. And, when the fuck did we go back to being teenagers?*

**Jack:** *Fuck off*

**Me:** *No, that's what YOU'LL be doing tonight.*

**Jack:** *Truth :(*

I laughed and stuck my phone back in my pocket, turning back to Bailey and giving her my full attention. We sat at the bar chatting for over half an hour before I led her to a quiet booth in the back. For another two hours, we talked about our jobs, friends, childhood—pretty much anything. I learned she was a third-grade teacher, was still best friends with a girl she went to high school with, and had grown up with a single mom. I couldn't hear enough, soaking up every little morsel she gave me.

After our third drinks, we both switched to water. There was something about this girl that had my mind wandering to sweaty, naked bodies wrapped up in sheets. I was going to do my best to make those vivid daydreams a reality, and I wanted her sober so she would remember every second.

At some point, I'd scooted across the booth to get as near to her as possible, under the pretense of hearing her over the noise of the music and people. Sitting so close, I could smell her strawberry scent and see the sprinkling of freckles across her nose. She was wearing a loose black sweater which drooped off one shoulder, revealing light freckles there as well. I wanted to connect the dots with my tongue and continue down until I knew where every single one was on her body.

Our conversation lulled and we stared at each other, the silence thick and heavy with want. Her eyes were filled with need, so I closed the distance between us and gently placed my mouth on hers. Her lips immediately parted, and I left gentle behind as my tongue swept in to mate with hers, my head slanting to deepen the kiss. I dove a hand into her lustrous hair and the other landed on her hip, bringing our bodies as flush as possible considering we were seated side by side. The air heated up, and I was no longer satisfied with the angle of our bodies, so I grasped her hips and started to lift her over to straddle me—

*Bang!*

I jerked back at the loud crack and Bailey's muffled cry of pain as she flopped back down beside me, cursing and rubbing her knee. She'd obviously hit it on the wooden table.

"Well, that was smooth," I drawled sarcastically, causing Bailey to giggle. "How about we try that again?"

Bailey eyed the tabletop skeptically. "I hate to break it to you Casanova, but I think the booth wins this round." She glanced around as though just remembering where we were. "Besides, I think the direction we were headed was bound to end up with us getting arrested for public indecency." She laughed and shook her head ruefully.

"You're right," I agreed. "I'm a much bigger fan of private indecency." I leaned down and put my face in the crook of her neck, nibbling my way up to her ear. "How about we try this again somewhere else?"

Bailey tilted her neck, giving me better access to the column of her throat. Damn, she tasted so fucking delicious.

"Um, what did you"—she gasped when I lightly bit her skin and grabbed onto my biceps—"have in mind?"

I licked the spot and whispered, "My house. I live about ten minutes from here."

Her chin bumped my head when she nodded, and I sat back to make sure I wasn't assuming anything. Her pink lips were puffy and a little red from rubbing against my scruff. She looked hot as hell.

"Bailey?"

There was uncertainty floating in her blue depths, a slight nervousness too. I hesitated, worried that I'd misread the situation. She leaned forward and dragged my bottom lip between her teeth, before letting it go and searing me with her blazing eyes. "Ten minutes?" I nodded. "That's an awfully long time."

I groaned, forgetting whatever it was I had been thinking and adjusted myself, grabbed her hand, and hauled her up from the booth. I was hard as a fucking rock and only sinking between her thighs was going to give me any relief. She stopped and pulled her phone from her purse to send a text. "Just letting my best friend know where I'm going and who I'm with."

I'd only known her a few hours, but I was proud of her for being safe and smart. *That's my girl.* I shook my head at the sudden thought, surprised when it didn't freak me the fuck out.

## Chapter 2

## WYATT

Not wanting to lose my chance with her, I hurried Bailey out to my jeep, helped her in, and jogged around to the driver's side. Once I was inside and the door was shut, I turned and tugged her toward me for a deep kiss. The parking lot of Jumpin' Jacks was not where I wanted to take her the first time. *That's right, first, because it certainly wouldn't be only once.* I dragged myself away, and we both buckled up before I peeled out of the parking lot and drove like a bat out of hell to my place.

After a few minutes, Bailey reached over and slid my zipper down. I sucked in a ragged breath when she slipped her hand in to grab my dick. "Baby, you're not helping the situation and unless you want to be fucked against the wall the minute we enter my house, you should be a good girl and keep your hands to yourself."

She didn't say anything, and I assumed she would do as I'd suggested until I felt her warm palm caress the aching head of my cock. A guttural groan ripped from my chest, and I thanked every fucking star in the sky that I squealed into my driveway at that moment.

Bailey didn't wait for me, we both unbuckled and threw open our doors, slammed them shut and raced to the house. I caught her on the top step and managed to fuse our mouths together as I unlocked the door. We tumbled inside, almost falling to the ground, barely managing to stay upright. She pushed me against the wall and attacked my mouth with a vengeance. After a few minutes of letting her hold the reins, I took over, twisting to push her back and bending to glide my hands under her skirt and lift her up by her ass. Her round, firm, naked, mouthwatering ass. *A motherfucking thong.* Her legs wrapped tight around me, pressing her pussy against my aching cock. The heat and friction were my undoing. I wanted to feast on her body, savor her, but it would have to wait.

I separated our lips and rasped, "I hope you'll forgive me, baby. I need to fuck you fast and hard, to be inside you. Now. I'll make it up to you, I promise."

That look flashed in her eyes again, but it was gone so swiftly that I questioned if

I'd actually seen it. Crashing my mouth down over hers once again, I yanked down her underwear, tearing it in the process. I grabbed a condom from my pocket and pulled out my cock. I leaned back slightly and rolled on the condom one-handed, a talent I was supremely grateful for, then swiped a finger up her pussy. "Damn, you are so fucking wet. You're ready to take me, aren't you, baby?"

She whimpered, her eyes shut, and her head resting on the wall. I slipped a finger inside her and she froze for a second before her hips thrust up, taking my finger deeper. "Baby, you're tight as hell." Her pussy was being stretched by my single digit, and it made me pause, worried that it had been a long time and I would hurt her. "How long has it been?" I asked, my voice muffled because I was kissing a line down her cleavage.

"It's—um, it's been a long time coming," she panted.

I assumed she didn't understand my question and was referring to how the night seemed to take forever to get us to this point. I plunged my finger in a few more times, eventually adding another. She was dripping down my hand and my mouth watered at the thought of licking up all that sweet cream later. Removing my fingers, I brought them to my mouth and sucked them clean. "I knew you'd taste amazing," I grunted. "I'm going to eat that pussy later, feast on it until you're screaming for me to stop."

Bailey moaned and her hips bucked. I lined us up and slammed her down onto my cock until I was fully inside her. Something snapped along the way and Bailey cried out. Time stood still. *No way.* I had to have imagined it. I looked up at her face and knew I hadn't. Tears were streaming down her cheeks, and my heart thudded loudly in my ears.

"Bailey, were you a virgin?" I asked incredulously. There was no comprehension in my mind of how this woman was untouched. Then, a new feeling slithered into me, slowly growing, and expanding my chest until I thought it would burst.

"Yes," she sniffed.

The feeling solidified. It was a mixture of pride and possession. I'd never have believed it existed if I hadn't been experiencing it at that very moment, but I knew, without a doubt, that this woman was mine. She had never been with anyone else and she never would. I was claiming her, taking her, and I wouldn't allow anything to stand in the way of that.

"I wish you'd told me, baby. I would have been gentler."

She blinked, then narrowed her eyes. "Would you have fucked me at all, if you knew?"

I opened my mouth to tell her I would have, but the words stuck in my throat, I didn't know if I would have had the same realization or not. "Does it matter?" She shifted, and I clenched my jaw so hard I worried that my teeth would crack.

"Baby, don't—oh, fuck. Don't move!" I bit out and she froze. "I'm sorry, I'm holding on by the skin of my teeth right now. Are you still hurting?"

She shifted again and I couldn't stop myself from pressing into her even deeper.

"Oh!" she cried out. I paused, and she gripped my shoulders, her nails digging into my skin through my shirt. "Don't stop!"

Slowly, I withdrew and eased back in. She was so wet that there was very little friction besides the walls of her pussy clamping down and trying to keep me inside when I pulled back again. She inhaled sharply. "You ok?" I hissed, trying not to drown in the pleasure.

"Wyatt! Would you focus on the task at hand instead of analyzing my every movement and sound?"

I stifled a laugh, "yes, ma'am."

Setting up a soft rhythm, I worked myself in and out, trying to be gentle. A smack on the back of my head brought my gaze flying to hers. "I'm not fragile, Wyatt. You said you needed to fuck me fast and hard against the wall, you were so desperate for me."

"Baby, it's your first time, I have to be—" She cut me off, slamming her mouth down on mine, sucking on my tongue, and squeezing her legs around my waist, the walls of her pussy tightening at the same time.

"Fuck!" I yelled. My hips took on a mind of their own and they began to piston into her hot pussy, each lunge shoving me a little deeper, pushing her a little harder into the wall. Her pants turned to cries, and then to screams, the sound breaking me. I lost my ever-loving mind and began pounding into her until her screams mixed with my own rasping grunts. I was on the precipice, but I was determined she would get off first. I could feel her tensing and getting close, so I pinched a nipple between my thumb and forefinger, twisting and pulling as I released it, then did the same to the other. She bucked wildly in my arms, "That's it, baby," I whispered roughly. "Let it go, let your pussy suck my cock so tight I'll never get it out. Come, baby." As I spoke, my hand slipped between us and just as I drove in with all of my strength, I pinched her clit. She went off like a motherfucking rocket. Screaming my name so loud, my ears were ringing, and I gripped her ass, thrusting one last time, leaving no space between us when I came, the strongest orgasm I'd ever had exploded inside her.

Twisting again, I slid to the floor, my ass hitting the ground and eliciting another groan as gravity brought Bailey down onto me and I realized I was still semi-hard. Our breathing finally started to calm, and I managed to lift her off of me, stand, and scoop her into my arms. She sighed blissfully, and I'm positive that if I'd been wearing a shirt with buttons, they would have been popping right off. We reached the bathroom, and I set her down on the sink before turning on the shower. When I went to remove the condom, the smeared blood on it reminded me that I had just fucked a virgin. Damn it! I cursed myself up one side and down the other for my lack of self-control. She was going to be sore as hell. I figuratively waved goodbye to my plan of marathon sex as it flew out the window.

Grabbing a cloth, I wet it with warm water and lifted Bailey's skirt, so I could clean and sooth her pussy. She winced a couple of times, and I felt like scum for taking her like I had. "Stop it."

Her voice brought me out of my thoughts as I tossed the rag into the trash. "Stop what, baby?"

"Stop regretting it."

My brows shot up. "You think I regret fucking you?" I clarified disbelievingly.

She pursed her kiss swollen lips, her blue eyes shuttered by her long eyelashes. "Don't you?"

I stepped between her legs and scooted her ass to the edge of the counter. With a single finger, I lifted her chin so that I could meet her gaze. "I will never, never, regret being with you, Bailey Cross. Do you understand?" My voice was firm, leaving no room for misinterpretation. She nodded, and I gave her a quick kiss. "I'm regretting the way I took you. You're likely going to be in a lot of pain tomorrow. I should have been—"

"Wyatt, stop," she interrupted. "It was perfect. Any pain I have to deal with tomorrow will be completely worth it."

I grinned, I couldn't help it. "So, it was good for you, huh?"

She smacked my chest playfully, then kissed me passionately. "Epic."

The shower was steaming up the bathroom, so I quickly undressed and helped Bailey out of her clothes. She blushed shyly when she was naked and hopped into the shower, making me laugh. "Baby, I've been deep inside you, now I want to enjoy the package on the outside."

I stepped under the hot spray and snuggled her back into my chest. Then I began a slow exploration of her curves, learning every soft inch of her delectable body, with my hands and my mouth. I discovered I was right—Bailey tasted like strawberries and cream, and her cream was the sweetest I'd ever tasted. The look of Bailey when she orgasmed? Nothing would ever compare.

The water eventually cooled and we washed up and stepped out of the glass enclosure. I wrapped a soft, emerald green towel around my waist and used another to dry Bailey before sweeping her into my arms and carrying her to my bed. Setting her down, I stood back and took in the view. Her copper hair spread out and glowing against the white pillows. Her round, large tits with their dusky nipples, small waist, plump hips, and long, long legs. Fucking gorgeous.

I crawled over her and lowered my body so we were flush, skin to skin. Damn, she felt good underneath me. Spearing a hand through her damp curls, I pulled them away from her face and placed soft kisses all over her face.

"There is something between us, baby. I can feel it tethering us together. This is more than one night. You know that, right?"

Bailey's answer was to kiss me senseless, driving every logical thought out of my brain. The passion began to burn hot, rapidly building into a frenzy of need. I tried to stop, suggested we go to sleep, warning her that she was already going to be incredibly sore. But, she had a way of convincing me to do just about anything she wanted. After rocking her world (not cocky...*confident*) with two more orgasms, I lost myself inside her once more.

Sweaty and sated, I fell over onto my back, taking her with me, staying snug inside her. Her breathing slowed, beginning to even out. I wrapped my arms around her and held on. There was one thing she wouldn't be able to get me to do. Let her go.

I gently squeezed her and a sweet little sigh fell from her lips. "I think I'll keep you."

Sunlight slashed across my face, the bright rays warm but keeping me from staying asleep. *Bailey.* The night before came rushing back and I smiled, then reached out to pull her soft body into mine. My hand met nothing but sun warmed sheets. I frowned and opened one eyelid, disgruntled that she'd gotten out of bed before I could wrap myself around her naked body and kiss her awake.

"Bailey?" I sighed and lifted up onto an elbow, opening both eyes and looking around the room. I didn't hear the shower running, but I climbed out of bed and padded over to the bathroom. Her clothes were no longer on the floor and mine had been folded and placed on the marble countertop. The open box of condoms near the sink reminded me that I'd fallen asleep still buried inside her. When I pulled off the condom I noticed a big tear right at the tip. *Fuck! The motherfucking condom broke! Shit. Shit. Shit.* I took a deep breath and washed my hands. OK, this wasn't so bad. She was mine, I would be marrying her and starting a family at some point. I just hadn't counted on doing it backwards.

I wondered briefly if Bailey had noticed when she'd gotten up. Then I dismissed the thought. If she had, I'd probably be attempting to calm her down from a panic attack right now. Where was she? "Baby?" I called, grabbing my robe and walking out to the kitchen. When I didn't find her there, I called her name again and checked every room. Something akin to dread was stabbing me in the chest, I stalked back to the bedroom, looked around and didn't find even a note. She must have called a cab and ducked out while I was sleeping. I started pacing, I needed a plan. All I had to go on was her name and the fact that she was only in town temporarily. *Fuck!*

"Bro, are you still moping?"

I scowled at Jack as he handed me a beer and flopped down next to me on my couch.

"Shut the fuck up, Jackass," I growled. I took a deep pull from the bottle and dropped my head back, blowing out a frustrated breath.

"No luck finding her, huh?" Jack asked, genuine sympathy in his voice this time. "You're going to have to let mystery girl go at some point. Why don't we go out tonight? We'll hit the bar and pick up some buxom blondes." He wiggled his eyebrows suggestively.

"I'm done with that scene, Jack. I'm serious." I gripped the bottle, my knuckles turning white. "She's mine. I refuse to accept any other outcome than to find her."

I'd practically shut down my life for the last month, working and searching. I'd exhausted most of my options. There were literally over four hundred people with the last name Cross in Nebraska. Narrowing it down by the first initial B didn't do me any good either. Not to mention, I didn't even know if her permanent residence was in the same state. I'd only spoken to Jack briefly, shortly after the morning Bailey had run out on me. He'd recently discovered that he had a half-sister and the family had been busy getting to know each other. Not that I was even ready to really talk about her with him anyway.

"Wow. Okay," Jack shrugged. "I guess you were serious about that."

I didn't reply, just chugged down the rest of my beer. I needed to get my mind on something else for a little while.

"How are things with the new sister?"

Jack's face softened, a look I never thought I'd see from him. "She fits right in. Honestly, I wish I'd been there to be her big brother growing up. She's beautiful, sweet and innocent and I get the feeling that I would have broken quite a few noses, maybe a jaw or two."

I laughed, the sound rusty and foreign to my ears. It felt good.

"Why don't you come have dinner with the family and meet her? Dad would love to see you." Jack rolled his eyes and chugged his beer. "And Sharon. She'd love to see you, all of you."

I snorted. Jack's step-mother Sharon was a unique species. She loved his dad, and was faithful, but she had no problem ogling "man candy," and wasn't shy about asking to see the "good stuff." She'd even used a drawing class excuse to try and get me to pose naked for her. She was...interesting. Harmless.

"So?" he queried.

"Sure, why not?" I agreed. I could use a night off from refining my pining and drinking abilities. I didn't intend to go pro, so all this practice was truly unnecessary.

"Great." Jack slapped me on the back and stood. "Oh, and when you meet Bailey, remember broken noses and jaws."

My eyes stopped mid-roll and I started choking on the swig of beer I'd just taken. Did he say...?

I coughed. "What's your sister's name?"

Jack was walking out the door but yelled back, "Bailey."

## Chapter 3

### Bailey

"I've been here a month, don't you think it's time you went back to your own home? Dad told me you didn't even spend this much time here when you were in high school."

*Dad.* It was crazy weird to toss that word out there in everyday conversation when I would have given anything to have been able to talk about my dad when I was growing up. I'd loved my mom more than anything in the world, but I'd missed out on so much by not having him around. When she was diagnosed with breast cancer my senior year of high school, I let go of my yearning to know about my father and focused on taking care of her. I changed all my plans and switched to a local college, staying at home instead of in the dorms so I could care for her.

Things were looking up by the time I graduated with my bachelor's degree and teaching license. Mom was nearing the five year anniversary of her last chemotherapy treatment, and I quickly landed a position at the elementary school I'd attended as a child. Then we got the call that changed our lives—again. The breast cancer hadn't come back, but she was diagnosed with leukemia, a side effect of the original treatment she'd received.

It was a battle she lost this time around, and she made a deathbed confession that left me reeling. She'd never told my father about her pregnancy. When they met, he'd been a widower with a young son, and she was fresh out of a broken relationship. They found comfort in each other while they healed, but it had never been a love match. She'd discovered she was pregnant after she'd moved away and decided it was better to keep the ties severed and uncomplicated.

When she realized she wasn't going to survive the leukemia, she hired a private investigator to locate him so I'd have the chance to meet him, if I wanted to. Less than three months later, here I was, sitting on the couch with my older brother in our dad's home in Nebraska—still struggling with the fact that my mom had kept me from them my entire life.

"Hey." Jack flicked my ear to gain my attention. "Do you want to get rid of me so much that you're going to ignore me now?"

"Sorry," I sighed. "I got lost in my head for a minute there, thinking about my mom."

His grin quickly turned into a grimace. My mom was a topic of conversation we avoided since he and my dad pretty much hated her for the decision to keep her pregnancy a secret. But, they respected my grief and the fact that, no matter what, she was still my mother, enough to keep their opinions mostly to themselves. As much as I loved her, I couldn't defend what she'd done. Not after what she'd cost all of us.

I needed to steer the discussion back on track because I didn't want to ruin everyone's dinner. "So what were you saying that was so important you needed to inflict bodily harm on me?"

He raised his hands up, palms facing me, an innocent expression on his handsome face. "Who? Me? I'd never hurt my sister."

"Uh-huh," I drawled, slugging him lightly on the arm. "Lucky for me, I never said anything about not hurting my brother."

"Hey!" he protested, rubbing the spot I'd hit. "No fair. It's a good thing I've got reinforcements coming."

"Reinforcements?"

"That's what I was trying to tell you. You finally get the chance to meet my best friend, little sis. But don't worry, I warned him to keep his hands to himself." He winked, and I forced a laugh.

Unless his name was Wyatt Kincaid, Jack didn't need to worry about his best friend ever getting the chance to touch me. That man had somehow managed to worm his way into my subconscious in the hours we'd spent together my first night in town. I'd spent every night after dreaming about him and the things he'd done to my body. "You don't need to warn all your friends away from me. I'm a grown ass woman. I can take care of myself."

"I'm sure you can with most guys, and I have a friend or two who I might, maybe, consider not killing if you decided you liked them. But you'll just have to trust my judgment when it comes to my friends."

I rolled my eyes at his superior tone. "I'm sure I can resist the temptation of your best friend without your help."

"It doesn't mean I'm going to stop giving it," he murmured, standing up and dropping a kiss on my head at the sound of the knock on the front door.

"Perfect timing!" Sharon called, as she and my dad carried serving platters to the dining room table. Their home had an open floor plan, with the living room flowing into the dining room. The kitchen was separated from the living space by a granite island surrounded by bar stools on three sides where we'd eaten most of our meals. Apparently the arrival of Jack's best friend warranted a more formal meal.

I was staring at the pot roast, my stomach churning as the smell of cooked meat wafted my way when I heard my brother teasing his friend.

"Flowers? You shouldn't have, man," he joked. "Although I'm sure Sharon will appreciate them."

"They're not for Sharon."

*That voice. It couldn't be.* I stood up from the couch and swiveled my head to find him standing in the doorway staring at me with heated eyes, a bouquet of blue and burnt orange colored flowers in his hands. Jack's best friend was Wyatt, the man I'd given my virginity to a month ago?

*Holy shitballs.*

"What do you mean 'they're not for Sharon'?" Jack scratched his head, clearly confused. "Who else would they be for?" His gaze followed Wyatt's line of sight, straight to me.

"They're for Bailey."

"Why would you bring Bailey flowers?" Jack asked, his eyes darting between me and Wyatt while we stood there staring at each other.

Something seemed to click in place, and his eyes narrowed in suspicion, "What the fuck, Wyatt?" His hands were clenched so hard at his sides that I could see the whitening of his knuckles from where I stood. "I warned you before she even came into town," Jack growled. "My sister is off limits to you. No flowers. No dates. No hookups. So stop fucking looking at her the way you are right now because I'm about thirty seconds from throwing your ass out with all of the broken bones we talked about."

I stepped forward, intending to step between the two men—to intervene with my brother on Wyatt's behalf. Jack didn't know that we'd met before, and Wyatt hadn't known I was Jack's sister. The last thing I wanted was for them to fight over me. I didn't make it far before my head began to swim and my stomach, which had only been slightly upset minutes earlier, heaved. I felt the blood drain from my face as chills raced along my skin.

*Crap!* I wasn't sure I was going to make it to the bathroom in time.

I turned and raced from the room, heading down the hallway as quickly as I could. Throwing the door open, I fell to my knees in front of the toilet and puked up my guts. At least, that's what it felt like I was doing. I'd never felt this badly before, not even the one time I'd had food poisoning from bad seafood when I was in college.

"Urg," I gagged in embarrassment when I realized Jack and Wyatt were standing in the doorway staring at me. Or more accurately, my brother was staring while he held Wyatt back from entering the bathroom.

"Don't just stand there, boys. Get out of the way unless you're going to help." My dad yanked on their collars like they were still little boys and dragged them backwards until Sharon was able to get past them.

"There's no way I'm going in there," Jack replied. "I don't want to catch whatever Bailey's got. You know how much I hate to puke."

"It's okay, honey," Sharon cooed as she grabbed a washcloth and ran it under cold water.

Wyatt was still trying to push his way into the bathroom. "You're not going to catch what she has."

I moaned in gratitude when Sharon wiped my face with the cool washcloth, but it turned into a groan of mortification when Jack piped back up again. "How the hell do you know I won't catch it?"

"Because she's pregnant, you asshole."

"Pregnant?" Jack and I repeated in unison.

My dad let go of the guys and came into the bathroom, squatting down so we were face-to-face, his eyes full of concern. "Is Wyatt right? Could you be pregnant, baby girl?"

My gaze darted over his shoulder to Wyatt, and images of our night together raced through my head. My cheeks heated at the carnal knowledge in his eyes. I dropped my head, staring at the floor while I did a quick calculation of the days in my head. Then I admitted a truth I hadn't considered until this moment—to my dad and to myself. "Yes, it's possible."

"Don't say it like being pregnant is the end of the world," Sharon chided. "Having a baby is the beginning, silly girl."

"How the fuck did you make the leap from her puking her guts up to a possible pregnancy?" Jack asked Wyatt. "And why did Bailey look at you the way she just did before answering the question?"

"It's okay, Bailey," my dad reassured me, pulling me onto his lap and wrapping his arms around me. "I promise everything's gonna be just fine."

"Because the baby is mine." I felt his body stiffen at Wyatt's response.

It was as though time stood still for a minute, and nobody knew how to react to Wyatt's announcement. Sharon wasn't at a loss for words long, though.

"You got to see Wyatt naked?" She patted me on the back. "Nicely done, baby girl. I've been trying to check out his family jewels for years, and you were able to get up close and personal with them. Good job!"

I didn't have the energy to do anything but sit, wrapped in my dad's embrace, and watch over his shoulder when my brother finally figured out how he wanted to react. He punched his best friend straight in the face.

# Chapter 4

## WYATT

"Fuck!" My head snapped to the side as Jack's fist connected with my jaw. *Should have seen that one coming. It was either that or your nose.* I cupped the aching bone in my palm and felt a small sense of smugness that he was shaking out his hand, hissing in pain.

"You knocked up my baby sister?" he bellowed.

"Jack, I didn't know she was your sister when I slept with her." I winced as soon as the words left my mouth. *Wrong thing to say, dude. Probably a bad idea to remind him that you fucked his sister.*

I ducked just as his fist was headed for my nose.

"Boys!"

Twenty-eight years old and the sound of Jack's dad's stern voice still had us snapping to attention. Milo was one of the fun dads, but he also demanded respect and didn't put up with any bullshit. I hated whenever he looked at me with disappointment, it was worse than anger. He opened his mouth, no doubt about to lecture us, but the sound of retching caught our attention again.

This time, I shouldered my way in before anyone could stop me and dropped to my knees next Bailey. Sharon handed me the freshly dampened cloth and stood, patting me on the back as she scooted past. She'd swept Bailey's long red hair up into a clip thing, so I used my empty hand to rub soothing circles on her back.

When it seemed as though everything was out of her stomach, she leaned back, and I used the cloth to wipe her mouth before tossing it in the trash bin. Then I gathered her into my arms and pulled her onto my lap. Her head fell to my chest, clearly from exhaustion, so when Sharon handed me a toothbrush, I helped her brush before lifting her to the sink to rinse out her mouth. When she was done, I carried her out of the bathroom but was forced to a stop by Jack standing in my way. He reached out and tried to take her from me.

"I'll take care of her, asshole. She's *my* sister," he snarled.

I held her tighter to my chest. "She's *my* fiancée," I countered. His eyes bulged and his face started to turn a mottled red. I didn't have time for this bullshit. I marched around him into the living room and gently placed Bailey on the couch. Milo appeared at my side and handed her a small glass of something clear and carbonated.

She took a small sip, and I brushed her hair away from her face, frowning at how pale she looked. Her eyes were a little glazed but they were clearing and she was observing me with a speculative gleam in them.

Milo placed a heavy hand on my shoulder and gave it a little squeeze. "I'm glad we won't be needing to have that talk about you doing the right thing and marrying her, Wyatt," he muttered. "You make me proud."

"Over my dead body!" Jack interjected. He'd come up right behind me and grabbed my collar, attempting to hoist me off the ground. We were approximately the same height and weight, but he had the element of surprise on me and was able to drag me to my feet.

I got into his face. "I'd hate to have to hurt you, Jack," I threatened, "but Bailey and I are getting married. This is not up for discussion."

"Excuse me," Bailey's voice interrupted and our gazes swung her way. I was relieved to see some of the color returning to her cheeks, although some of the flush was clearly from anger. "I'm right here. So, first, don't talk about me as if I'm not. Second, I don't know for sure if I am pregnant, only that it's possible. And third, no one is getting married."

I blanched. "We sure as fuck are," I growled.

Milo put up his hand for silence, looking straight at me and Jack. Once again, we followed orders immediately. He knelt down by the couch and took Bailey's hand. "If you are pregnant—"

I snorted at the insinuation that she might not be.

"—then you need to get married, baby girl."

Bailey's eyes darted between Jack and Milo, her brows lowered, a frown marring her beautiful face.

"All those years wasted, Bailey. We could have been a family. You don't want to take that away from your son or daughter, do you?"

Bailey's eyes filled with tears. "No," she agreed, "but this isn't the same thing, Dad. Wyatt knows, and I have no intention of keeping them apart if there is a baby."

"Besides," Jack huffed, "she has us now. She doesn't need a fair-weather husband who wouldn't know commitment if it bit him in the ass."

One more comment and so help me, I was going to staple his mouth shut.

"Jack!" Milo snapped. "You're not helping."

Bailey's watery eyes were fastened on Jack, a flash of fear darkening the ocean blue.

"Jack is right, though, isn't he?" she asked in a whisper, looking back at her dad. "I have my family to support me." I'd never seen Milo wear the expression that came over his face, she was clearly precious to him, and it notched up my admiration for him in every way.

"Of course, baby girl. No matter what you decide, we'll be here for you." His countenance suddenly perked up, his face hopeful. "Does this mean you'll move here permanently?"

This whole discussion was ridiculous and it was starting to piss me off. I didn't know where she was visiting from, but I'd be moving her ass here and into my house as soon as possible. We were getting married and could get to know each other as man and wife. Besides, I already knew she was my forever, and now that we were having a baby, it would be easier to convince her.

"Of course, she'll move here," I barked. "My wife and baby will be living with me."

Bailey glared at me, and I just shrugged. This wasn't up for debate, it was the way it was going to be, damn it.

# Chapter 5

## Bailey

I didn't appreciate how a man I barely knew thought he could make decisions about my life for me. Unless you counted carnal knowledge because he certainly had that in spades. I shook my head, trying to focus on anything but the images of how he gained that knowledge.

"We don't even know if there is a baby," I argued, my focus wholly on Wyatt as my dad stood and moved away to let him get closer to me. Sure, my period was late, and the smell of pot roast had just made me puke my guts up, but it could be something else. *Right?* "I could have picked up a stomach bug or eaten something which didn't agree with me."

Wyatt's gaze dropped to my belly and then moved back up to my face to meet mine. "You didn't catch anything except my baby."

I lowered my voice to the barest whisper, not wanting my dad or brother to hear any of the details about the night I'd spent with Wyatt. "But you wore a condom both times."

He crouched down in front of me, taking my hands in his and matching his tone to mine. "It broke, baby. I didn't realize until I woke up in the morning." His hold tightened, almost as though he was afraid I'd move away from him. "I would have talked to you about it sooner, but you pulled a vanishing act on me."

His evident frustration surprised me. It had been hard to leave his home that morning, but I figured it was what I was supposed to do—what he expected from me. I'd acted completely out of character with him, but even while I was freaking out about the situation, I'd felt safe wrapped up in his arms. I hadn't intended to hurt him, but I was starting to think that's exactly what I'd done. Maybe I should have listened to my best friend's advice and gone back to his house the next day. She'd screeched so loudly in my ear while yelling at me for running out on him like that during our call that I'd thought I might go deaf. "I'm sorry. I didn't think you'd want me there for the whole awkward morning after thing."

"You thought wrong, Bailey," he growled, his voice rising slightly. "I wanted you there that morning and every one after."

"Sure you did," Jack hissed.

My head jerked up, his interjection surprising me because I'd somehow managed to forget my brother and dad were in the room with us. My fascination with him was just that absolute.

"Stop saying shit to make your sister doubt me," Wyatt tossed over his shoulder before turning back to me. "Do you know how many Cross families there are in the state of Nebraska? Because I do."

"How?" I gasped.

"I've spent the last month looking for you, Bailey." It was impossible to doubt the sincerity of his statement. At least it was for me. My brother was an entirely different matter.

"This is bullshit."

My dad stepped forward and pulled Jack back a few steps. "He's your best friend, Jack. You've known each other forever, and you and I both know he's a good man. I get that being a big brother is new to you, just like having a daughter to protect is for me, but we both need to let Bailey and Wyatt talk this through without making the situation harder for them."

"We don't even know if we have a situation yet," I groaned, utterly mortified by the whole conversation.

"And that's where I come in," Sharon said from the front door, shutting it behind her. I hadn't even realized she'd left, but she held a bag from the drug store down the street in her hand. She walked over and dropped it into my lap. "Since your best friend isn't in town, I figured it was my responsibility as your step-mom to run out and buy you a pregnancy test."

Gripping the bag tightly in my fist, I jumped up from the couch and hugged Sharon. There was no way I could make it through the day without finding out if I was pregnant. Heck, I didn't even know if I could make it another hour, and now I didn't have to because of her. I raced back into the bathroom and dumped the contents of the bag onto the counter. There were three different kinds of tests. Who even knew there were so many types available? Scanning the back of each one, I decided to use the one which offered the most obvious result. No pluses or lines for me. I wanted the test that promised to provide early results with the words "pregnant" or "not pregnant" on the display.

I ripped open the box and started to turn towards the toilet when I caught a glimpse in the mirror of Wyatt's reflection. He was standing in the doorway watching me. "Nope. No way." I nudged him back a step. "You can wait out there. I'm not going to pee in front of you."

I shut the door gently, resisting the urge to slam it in his face. It wasn't his fault the condom broke. I'd been a willing participant in everything we'd done together. My hand dropped to my belly, rubbing lightly, as I walked back to the toilet. I did my business and laid the stick back on the counter. Then I leaned against the door, wanting to be closer to Wyatt but not quite ready to open it and see him yet. My pulse was racing, and my stomach was turning again as I waited for the results to come in. Three minutes never seemed to last quite so long. And then it was over and the results were in.

*Pregnant.*

I was pregnant.

*Ohmigod I was pregnant.*

With Wyatt's baby.

And he was waiting right outside that door.

"There's no time like the present," I whispered to myself before pulling the door open.

Wyatt was standing right there, a shit-eating grin on his face. "I knocked you up, right?"

"You're not supposed to look so happy about it," I grumbled. "Besides which, these tests aren't one hundred percent accurate. I should probably find a doctor so I can get a blood test to confirm it."

His grin turned even more smug and he picked me up and spun me around.

"Put the girl down before you make her sick again," Sharon chided.

She had a good point because my head was already spinning, and not in shock. This was the light-headed kind where you ended up with black spots dancing in front of your eyes. "No joke."

"Sorry, baby. I should know better. I promise to do better from now on." He placed me gently on the couch. "Starting with getting you in to see a doctor today."

When Wyatt put his mind to something, he got things done, and fast. It was only forty-five minutes later when I found myself in the doctor's office being ushered back to an exam room with Wyatt by my side.

"The doctor will be in shortly. Go ahead and get into a gown, ties in the front, panties off but you can leave the bra on if you'd like," the nurse instructed, shutting the door behind her.

"Turn around." I circled my finger in the air at Wyatt.

"It's not like I haven't seen it all before," he grumbled, but turned and faced the wall as I'd asked. "Touched, licked and sucked it, too."

"Yeah, you did," I mumbled under my breath, blushing at the memories while I finished changing into the gown and climbed onto the exam table.

"What?" Wyatt asked.

"I said you can turn around now," I totally lied.

"You sure that's what you said?"

I was saved by a quick knock on the door. The nurse from before peeked her head inside. "Hey, the doctor is running a little behind and wanted me to get your blood draw started. Are you decent?"

"I am," I confirmed.

She came into the room, followed by a phlebotomist. Wyatt held my other hand while she took a few samples for testing. "Why so many tubes to test for pregnancy?" he asked.

"As long as we're doing a needle stick, we'll check for other things, too. Nothing to worry about. It's standard. If Bailey's pregnant, she'll end up getting stuck so many times, she'll appreciate us doubling up now."

"Great," I muttered when we were alone again. "I hate needles."

He released my hands, toying with the hem of the gown—and making me want to spread my legs and wrap them around his hips, as inappropriate as it would be to actually do. "Then I guess it'll be my job to make each trip to the doctor worthwhile."

I had a pretty good idea based on the circles his thumbs were drawing on my knees, but I couldn't resist asking anyway. "How, pray tell, will you do that?"

"Like this," he whispered as he slid his hands up my thighs until they rested just below my pussy. "By making you come for me."

He pressed down firmly, widening my legs and opening me to his touch. I was already wet and hot, all it had taken was the feel of his palms on my bare legs. My hips lifted as his fingers swirled in a circle over my clit.

"We can't do this," I protested feebly. "The doctor could be here at any moment."

"Then I guess I'd better work fast to get you off before he knocks on the door because it's bad enough that he's a guy. There's no fucking way I'm going to let him see how gorgeous you are when you come."

His touch on my clit became more demanding and he slid a finger inside me.

"I'm so close," I moaned.

He twisted his hand, finding just the right spot, but that wasn't what sent me over the edge. It was the way he looked at me when he leaned his head against mine and watched me fly apart in his hands.

Seriously, who was I when I was with Wyatt? How did he manage to make me forget everything to the point of finding myself spread-eagle on the exam table of my step-mother's OBGYN's office, the awful gown riding up my legs, while I climaxed on his hand?

## Chapter 6

## WYATT

There was nothing in this world as beautiful as Bailey when she comes. I pulled my finger from the suction of her soaked pussy and keeping my eyes locked on hers, licked it clean. Her face heated with a blush and I winked, a smirk playing on my lips.

There was a short rap on the door before it slowly opened. "Bailey Cross?" A middle-aged man in a white lab coat entered, looking over a chart, before taking a seat on a small stool at the bottom of the examination table. When he glanced up from the paper, he frowned, "Are you feeling alright, Ms. Cross? You look a little flushed, are you overly warm?" he asked as he grabbed a thermometer from the table of instruments beside him.

I stifled a laugh and Bailey shot me a murderous glance, making it even harder to hold it in.

"I'm fine, thank you, doctor," she said quickly. "I'm simply nervous."

He appeared doubtful, but put the machine back down, returning to her chart. "First, let me confirm, you are pregnant."

My grin felt like it was going to split my face. This was everything I could've hoped for. I was ecstatic to find out I was going to be a dad, but the added benefit was that Bailey was now permanently tied to me. Plans started to form in my head, moving her in, a quick wedding, making her fall in love with me. I'd fallen for Bailey the moment I met her and I was going to make sure she needed me as much as I did her.

She still looked a little shell-shocked, but her eyes were also lit with happiness and I sighed in relief. The doctor poked and prodded her a bit then went over some information with us, vitamins, approximate due date, and a list of do's and don'ts. When he was done, he set down the chart and turned on the computer looking machine next to the instrument table. "Would you and your husband like me to do an ultrasound? We may not be able to see anything, but sometimes the baby will make an appearance this early."

"Oh, we're not married," Bailey immediately clarified, which ticked me off.

"Yet," I grumbled, "We're not married yet, but we're engaged."

Bailey opened her mouth, most likely to argue, but shut it when I glared at her, grunting in irritation instead.

"Yes, we'd like an ultrasound," I answered for her.

The doctor stood and reached for one of the ties on my woman's gown. Knowing she had no panties on, I unintentionally growled and he stepped back in surprise.

Bailey rolled her eyes. "Can I slip my underwear back on first?" she asked sweetly.

"Oh, um yes, go ahead."

The doctor busied himself with something while Bailey hopped off of the table to get her panties. I found them first and attempted to help her put them on, ignoring her when she slapped my hands away. She gave up and stepped into them as I crouched, holding them out for her. I slid them up her legs, letting my fingers trail over her silky skin, just managing not to press my face between her cleft and inhale deeply. A little whimper escaped her lips and I grew so hard, I was worried I wouldn't be able to leave the office without fucking her. I couldn't wait to get her home so I could reacquaint myself with her delectable body.

The doctor coughed awkwardly, breaking into our moment. I stood and lifted Bailey back onto the table. He hesitantly reached out again but she opened the gown first, glancing at me with annoyance. I shrugged and took her hand. I wouldn't apologize for the possessive feelings I had for her.

When her stomach was visible, I stared at it in wonder. Looking a little closer, I was sure I could see a slight rounding of the area, just barely there, but I latched onto the fact that my girl was now sporting a baby bump.

Pointing at it, I excitedly asked the doctor, "I'm not imagining that, right?"

Bailey's head flew up from where it had been resting, her hand fastened on her stomach. She ran a hand over the not quite flat surface and groaned, despite the delighted sparkle in her baby blues. "How didn't I notice that?"

The doctor chuckled, "It's easy to miss if you aren't looking for it. The fact that there is evidence of pregnancy this early means we may be more likely to see the baby on the scan."

After squirting some goo on her stomach, he moved a wand-type thing over the area and watched the screen on the monitor.

The screen lit up and the doctor moved the instrument around her belly. He finally paused and used one latex glove covered finger to tap the screen. "That little black blob among all the white is where your little one is growing."

My eyes were glued to the image in front of me, my hand gripping Bailey's firmly. The doctor leaned over to hit a button, breaking my connection to the machine. I used a single finger under her chin to turn Bailey's head toward me. I'm positive that the wonder on her face was reflected on mine. I leaned down and brushed my lips over hers. "That's our kid, baby." She nodded silently and I kissed her again, lingering until I heard the doctor clear his throat.

We gave him our attention and he handed us two small photos, capturing the moment when we first saw our little peanut. I took them reverently and after staring at them a little longer, I put one in Bailey's purse and slid the other into my wallet.

"You should make an appointment to see your OBGYN in six weeks, or if you decide to continue with me, Lisa, at the front, will help you book it."

He stripped off the gloves and shook our hands then left us alone. I helped Bailey off of the table and turned to let her dress without argument, both of us lost in our thoughts.

She touched my arm to let me know it was safe to turn around, and I laced my fingers with hers as we left the room. We stopped at the front to pick up a prescription for vitamins and she mentioned to the woman behind the counter that she wanted to book her next visit.

*Not fucking happening.*

"She won't be needing another appointment. Thank you," I said tersely and dragged Bailey from the office, ignoring her sputtering.

"What the heck, Wyatt?" she yelled when we reached the car.

Opening her door, I lifted her onto the passenger seat of my truck and buckled her in before answering. "Baby, we'll find you the best doctor in town. *The best female doctor,*" I stressed. Then I shut the door and loped around to the driver's side.

Bailey huffed a little and muttered something about bossy men. She could complain all she wanted, I was the *only* man who would ever be spending time with her pretty pussy.

Once we were out on the road, I drove toward my house with urgency, desperate to be buried balls deep into my girl.

"Wyatt, you missed the turn-off," she said impatiently when I drove right by her dad's street.

"We're going home," my voice was matter-of-fact.

"*My* home is back there," she objected, her thumb jerking back over her shoulder.

I sighed, "We'll discuss living arrangements later. Let me put it this way"—my hand automatically went between her legs and pressed against her center—"Baby, I've waited four weeks to fuck you again and I'm not waiting any longer to own this pussy," I drawled. "It's either our house, your dad's, or this truck. Take your pick."

Rubbing my hand a little harder, I mentally crowed in triumph when she panted, "Yours," followed by a needy moan.

I hit the gas a little harder and slipped a finger inside her drenched panties. I almost laughed at the similarity of this situation to when we met. We pulled into my driveway and I threw the truck into park, then raced around to her side and unbuckled her before she had the chance. Her hand tucked in mine, I dragged her to the house and unlocked the door, pulling her inside and kicking it closed as I pressed her back into the wall.

"Thinking about what I did to you against this wall," I murmured, nibbling on her ear. "Making you mine and only mine, I'm tempted to reenact it all over again." My hips rocked into hers as I took her mouth in a deep, thorough kiss, feeling her body tremble. "Another time. I need you in our bed."

I picked her up and threw her over my shoulder in a fireman's hold, stalking down the hall to the bedroom.

"Your bed," I heard her grumble softly, earning a hard smack on her luscious ass.

"Ow!" she exclaimed, wiggling to get out of my grip, but I tightened my hold, careful not to drop her.

When we got to my bed, I gently laid her on it and followed her down until my body completely covered hers. She was so damn soft, generous curves without any bony angles I'd be afraid of cutting myself on. I was about at my end, so I shoved my hand down her pants and under her panties, my finger plunging and finding her so fucking wet and ready for me.

I whipped my shirt off and slipped hers over her head, my cock practically weeping at the sight of her large tits. Sealing my mouth over hers, I managed to keep the contact as I stripped us both down to nothing. The contact of our naked, feverish bodies drew guttural groans from each of us.

"You're so fucking perfect, baby. I'll never get enough of you." I dipped my head to suck one fat nipple into my mouth and grunted at the sweet taste. "I can't wait to see these swollen and full, ready to feed our kid."

Grabbing my rock hard cock, I squeezed the base once, trying to relieve some of the pressure so I wouldn't blow the minute I entered her. *Fuck it.* I let go and drove deep, so fucking deep. She cried out and the sound of it, mixed with the exquisite sensation of being inside her bare, spurred me into a frenzy. My mouth continued to feast on her tits, biting, sucking, and licking her nipples as I drove my dick into her pussy.

"Wyatt! Oh, oh! Don't stop!"

*Not a fucking chance in hell.*

Palming her perfect ass, I lifted her pelvis to change the angle and she began to scream with each push of my cock. The walls of her pussy were tightening, clenching, taking hold of me and trying to keep me deep inside.

"Fuck, baby. You feel so damn good. I could live in this tight, little pussy."

I was getting harder and a tingling started at the base of my spine as my balls began to draw up. *Not yet.*

"This pussy is mine, Bailey," I barked. "I was your first and I'm going to be your last. You belong here with me, in our house, our bed, giving me babies."

"Wyatt, you can't just—"

I cut her off, slamming in even deeper and when her whole body was trembling and she was screaming my name, I lifted one hand and spanked her ass, wishing I could see the red palm print on that plump cheek. One more slap and she splintered, her body convulsing and gripping me so damn tight. On my next thrust, I buried myself so deep inside her, I wondered if I'd permanently fused our bodies into one.

"Fuuuuuuuck!" I shouted, jets of come shooting from my body over and over, filling her with as much of me as possible. My orgasm was so fierce, I wondered if it was possible to have put another baby inside her.

Empty and spent, I collapsed on top of her but rolled to the side immediately so I wouldn't crush her. I flipped her around and tugged her into me so her back was plastered against my front. Throwing a leg over hers and wrapping her up tight in my arms, I fell asleep determined to keep her from running out on me in the morning.

# Chapter 7

## Bailey

I had a feeling of déjà vu when I woke up, wrapped in Wyatt's arms after another passionate night. The last time I'd been in this exact same spot, I'd freaked out and left before he realized I was gone. It was tempting to try it again, but I knew I wouldn't be able to go far. My conscience wouldn't let me, not when I was pregnant with his baby—and neither would he. He'd made that obvious when he'd told me he'd looked for me when I'd left before. I let it sink in for a moment.

*Wyatt looked for me.*

No, that was an understatement.

He'd searched the entire state of Nebraska trying to find me. *Me, the inexperienced virgin he'd fucked against a wall.*

Our situation was sudden, there was no arguing how quickly things had happened between us. The way I reacted to him was scary. Knowing I was pregnant with his baby was life-changing. But it was all a little bit thrilling, realizing a man like him wanted me so badly. Wyatt's leg slid between mine as he stirred, sending tingles up my spine. *Correction, our situation was panty-meltingly explosive.*

As tempting as it was to enjoy the feel of his warm body against mine, I needed to pee. Immediately. I was contemplating how to extricate myself from his hold to escape to the bathroom when my stomach let out the loudest growl in the history of the world. *Busted by my own belly.*

"Fuck," Wyatt groaned in a gravelly voice, his arms tightening around me. "I should have made sure you had a snack before we fell asleep. You barely touched your dinner and it sounds like my boy needs to be fed."

I couldn't argue the not eating much part because the smell of the pot roast had kept my stomach rolling last night. Apparently, I was in the night sickness phase instead of morning sickness because I was starving without a hint of nausea right now. But the boy part? Yeah, that I could argue. "I think you mean my girl needs breakfast."

He rubbed his chin against my neck, his stubble scraping against my tender skin and leaving goosebumps in its wake.

"You give me a baby girl and I just might have to spank your ass again."

My face heated at the reminder of how I'd reacted to the feel of his palm smacking against my skin last night. It had been insanely hot and now I was wondering if there was anything I could do to guarantee we had a girl. Getting a sexy spanking from Wyatt definitely wasn't a deterrent. I didn't want him to be aware of that little fact, though, since I wanted the chance to earn some ass taps in the future.

I decided a little sass might move it along. "Are you telling me you would love a son more than a daughter?"

"Of course not," he answered, clearly annoyed at my assumption. "But, boys I don't have to worry about. If our daughter was half as beautiful as her mommy, I'd have to lock her in a tower where boys can't get to her"—he paused, rubbing his chin thoughtfully—"A chastity belt wouldn't be out of the realm of consideration, either."

I rolled my eyes and laughed, but inside I was swooning. "How about you find me some food while I'm in the bathroom and we can worry about the sex of our baby later? I'm not even sure when we can find out what we're having." Holy crap, I was going to have a baby and I didn't know anything about pregnancy or being a parent. I'd never even held a baby before. "I need to go to the bookstore today."

"Bathroom, food and a bookstore," Wyatt chuckled. "I think I can manage all that for you, but not until I get my good morning kiss. I missed out on one last time and promised myself I would start all of my days with a kiss from you once I managed to find you. I didn't expect it to take so damn long, but now I'm more than ready to make up for all the mornings I missed."

He didn't give me a chance to object, cupping my face in his palm and tilting my head so he could capture my lips. It wasn't a closed lip, worried about morning breath kiss, either. This was an all-consuming, heart-pounding, forget about how much I needed to use the bathroom kiss. My legs were shaking so badly by the time he released me, I was barely able to stumble away from the bed.

My cheeks were still flushed and my lips swollen when I stared at myself in the mirror while washing my hands. I splashed cold water on my face, hoping to hide just how much his kiss had affected me. We had serious issues to discuss today, and Wyatt didn't need to know he had a secret weapon in his arsenal. With the way he made me melt, I needed all the advantages I could get, including a hearty breakfast to start my morning. A much needed one based on the painful, gnawing sensation in my stomach.

I wandered into the kitchen and found Wyatt standing in front of the fridge, his arm resting on the open door. "Feed me," I whimpered.

He turned to look at me, an apologetic look on his face while he shut the fridge door. "Remember when I promised you food?"

"Umm, yeah. It was only a couple minutes ago."

"We're going to have to go out for breakfast because there's practically no food in the house," he admitted. "Certainly nothing I'd feel safe serving to you since I'm not even sure how long any of the leftover containers have been in there."

I scooted past him and opened the fridge door, finding a pizza box, Chinese takeout containers and beer on the shelves. Glancing at the door, I noticed butter, milk and a bottle of syrup. "Breakfast might just be saved." I moved to the pantry, pulling open the door and searching the almost bare shelves for anything resembling pancake mix or flour. I let out a startled laugh, surprised to learn he didn't even have enough of the most basic staples on hand. The house might not look like it on the surface, but Wyatt's place was definitely a bachelor pad. "Scratch that, we're definitely going out to eat." My stomach growled loudly again. "Now."

I wasn't happy putting my clothes back on from the day before to head out the door early in the morning. I was even less so when Wyatt changed my order. "Switch her coffee to herbal tea and add a side order of fresh fruit."

The waitress shifted her attention back to me, her brow lifted and lips tilted in amusement. "That okay with you, sweetie?"

"I hate tea," I grumbled.

"Caffeine isn't good for the baby," Wyatt replied.

"Ahh, that explains it," the waitress laughed, her gaze dropping to my belly.

"How about I bring you decaf coffee instead? All the flavor with none of the lead."

"Fine," I sighed, complaining to Wyatt after she walked away. "The whole point of coffee is the caffeine."

"Baby," he replied like it was a complete answer. I guessed it kind of was, at least until I had a pregnancy book in hand which said I could have a cup of coffee without hurting the baby.

"Don't be a smartass."

"Better than a dumbass," he shot back.

Gah! Winning with this man was impossible. "Just so long as you don't think this means I'm going to start letting you make all my decisions for me."

He reached underneath my chair and scooted it closer to his, wrapping an arm around my shoulder once I was near enough. "I'll try my best to not steamroll over you, but I'm going to have a say in your life from now on."

I bit my tongue, wanting to argue but knowing it wasn't fair. To a certain extent, what he'd said was true. I was pregnant with his baby, which meant we were going to be connected forever, regardless of what happened between the two of us in the future. "I'll listen to your input," I conceded.

"Good." He nodded. "Because we need to talk about your living arrangements, and I have a lot of *input* I'd like to provide." He practically spat out the word 'input,' making his distaste for my word choice clear. "Starting with the fact that I want you to move here permanently."

"I'm not sure I'm ready yet."

He didn't let me finish my response. "I wasn't done yet, Bailey." His arm slid off my shoulder, and he turned me so we were facing each other. "When I say 'here,' I don't mean this town, and not your dad's place either. I want you under my roof so I can watch my baby grow in your belly, to be with you every step of the way."

I dropped my head against his chest and groaned. "How am I supposed to argue with you when you say such sweet things?"

"You aren't. It'll be much easier if you just go along with everything I want."

My head jerked back up at the sound of plates being set down on the table. "Don't go tricking the girl into agreeing to something when she's dying of hunger." The waitress shook her finger at him before turning her attention to me. "Go ahead and fill your belly so you can think straight before you tell him you'll do whatever he wants."

*Saved by the food.* Our conversation halted while I stuffed my face, eating all the food I'd ordered plus the fruit Wyatt had insisted on getting me. It gave me some time to mull things over, and I was ready to discuss things a little more rationally once I'd satisfied my hunger.

"When I came to Nebraska, it was only supposed to be for the summer. I wanted the chance to get to know my dad and brother, but I always planned to go back home before the school year started. I have a job and a home there waiting for me."

"That may be true, but you have a family and the father of your baby here for you," he pointed out.

I gripped his hand, lacing my fingers through his while I searched for the right words to make him understand. "For so long, it was my mom and I against the world. Now she's gone and I have a family." I paused, my hand dropping to my belly. "A growing one at that, but I'm not ready to let go of the house I spent my entire childhood in. It's the last tie to my mom and I'm not prepared to sell it and walk away."

"I'm not asking you to give up your mom's house," he murmured, resting his hand on mine. "We can keep it for family vacations, let our kids see what your childhood was like. Hell, we can spend the entire summer there each year if you'd like. I'm an architect, and my own boss since I own the firm. I can work from wherever I want with a mobile office, and the place I most want to be is by your side."

"There you go with the sweet again," I sighed, considering all that he'd said. The thought of returning to my hometown three months pregnant and alone except for my best friend was daunting. It wasn't what I wanted for myself, and it sure as heck wasn't what I wanted for my baby. Especially not when Wyatt was offering me the perfect solution. "I'll call the school and see if they'll give me a leave of absence due to the pregnancy. If I'm going to spend the next year—"

"More like the rest of your life," he interrupted.

I glared at him. "—here, then I'll need to go back and get some of my personal items and mementos I left back home.

Clothes won't be an issue since I'm going to need a whole new wardrobe anyway due to the pregnancy."

"I'll drive you out and load the truck myself if it means I'm moving it all into my house."

"Then I guess you have a deal," I agreed. "But don't think for a second that I've forgotten how you called me your fiancée at the doctor's office yesterday. I might have agreed to move in with you, but that doesn't mean I'm going to marry you."

"Maybe not yet," he replied, a smug grin on his face because he knew he'd won this round. "But I'm going to do whatever it takes to make it happen before you give birth to my child, and that's a promise you can take to the bank."

I felt like the gauntlet had been thrown down, but there was no way I was going to pick it up. It was a challenge I was pretty sure I couldn't win, not against the man who'd gotten me in his bed the first night we'd met. The same man who'd managed to knock me up the second time I'd ever had sex. And he'd been able to talk me into leaving the town where I'd grown up to move halfway across the country. He was persuasive, to say the least. Plus, if I was brutally honest with myself, I wasn't even sure I wanted to win.

# Chapter 8

## WYATT

I loaded one last box into my truck, shut the tailgate, secured the tarp, and returned to the house. We'd been in California two days gathering up Bailey's belongings. At first, she'd only packed another suitcase and a small box, as though she was coming back for an extended visit. I didn't let her get away with that. She may not have fully come to terms with it yet, but this was no longer her home. I started packing up her bedroom while she huffed in annoyance and stormed off. Taking my time, I worked slowly, waiting. Sure enough, not twenty minutes later, she stalked back into the room and shouldered me aside muttering that I was doing it all wrong.

I laughed and held up my hands in surrender until she gave me direction and we got to work. We completed the room the next day and she asked me to stack all of the boxes in a corner. I did as requested, but when she went to dinner with her best friend, I loaded it all into the back of the truck. I'd insisted on staying in a hotel, not wanting her to be cleaning up after us in addition to packing, so she didn't return to the house that night. I managed to keep her distracted enough that she didn't notice the boxes this morning as well and now I was ready to get on the road.

It was early afternoon and we'd be able to go a good distance before pulling off for the night. I didn't like having her sitting in the car for such long stretches, but I wanted to get her home and settled even more. I planned to stop early enough to have a relaxed dinner and get a good night's sleep, though. I was particularly dedicated to wearing her out so she wouldn't have any trouble sleeping.

I grinned to myself. Some nights, I collapsed before Bailey, she was insatiable. If this was how she would be every time she was pregnant, I was seriously considering keeping her knocked up for the next decade.

Once I walked in the front door, I stopped and watched her as she wandered around the front room, her hand softly trailing along, touching mementos and furniture. Her face was wistful, her eyes full of sadness, and I wanted nothing more than to take away the pain of her past. After a few minutes, I strode over and wrapped her up in my arms. She leaned against me, her head resting on my chest, and took a deep breath.

"She would have loved to be a grandma," she mumbled, then chuckled, the sound muffled against my t-shirt. "As crazy as it sounds considering what she pulled with my dad, she wouldn't have been so keen on me having a baby out-of-wedlock, though."

"Easily rectified." I reminded her. I'd been taking every opportunity to bring up getting married, but she'd been very adept at skirting the subject, much to my frustration.

She was silent for a bit, then she rubbed her nose on my shirt as though giving it an Eskimo kiss. "She would have liked you." Warmth spread through my chest at the idea that her mother would have approved of me. I was kind of hoping that she was rooting for me, wherever she was.

Bailey sniffed and it broke my heart knowing she was hurting. I wanted so badly to be able to change it, but there was no fixing this. I dropped a kiss on the top of her deep red curls, then rested my cheek on the silky spot.

"I'm sure our son would have adored her."

I felt her cheeks move up in a smile before I heard her sweet little laugh. "Yes, our daughter would have loved her grandma."

We'd been playing this game for days and I knew it would lighten her mood. I loved to tease her about the baby being a boy, but the truth was, the image of a beautiful baby girl with her mother's red hair and blue eyes had taken root in my head. However, it was accompanied by terror when I thought about her getting old enough to date. No boy would ever be good enough for my baby girl. Boys. We should only have boys.

"Are you ready to go, baby?" I kissed her head again when she sighed.

"Yes." She looked up at me and her ocean blue eyes were swimming with tears but she was giving me a tremulous smile. "It's hard to let her go, but I'm excited to have a wonderful new chapter starting in my life."

I took my arms from around her and cupped her cheeks in my palms, kissing away each tear that escaped. "I wasn't expecting our part of this story, baby. But, seeing it in front of me now, I couldn't be happier."

Lifting Bailey into my arms, I felt her stir as I carried her and our bag to the door of our hotel room. She'd fallen into an emotionally exhausted sleep about an hour into our drive. It wasn't late, but she was getting more and more tired lately. I was worried at first but I'd read the books Bailey bought, and they said it was normal.

I didn't want her uncomfortable, so once we got through Las Vegas, I stopped at a hotel and checked us in for the night. After getting into the room, I set the bag down and laid her gently on the bed. Looking her over, I was floored by her beauty, and a rush of possessiveness reminded me that she is mine.

I hated to wake her, but she and the baby needed to eat. I shook my head, still full of wonder at the fact that she was pregnant. And, I'd be honest, a healthy dose of male pride. *Way to go boys.*

Smoothing a hand over her brow, I placed a soft kiss on her lips and quietly said her name. "Bailey, it's time to wake up, baby. I need to feed you, then you can go back to sleep."

She stirred and her eyes fluttered open, gracing me with a sweet smile. "I'm so sorry, I'm a terrible road trip buddy," she said sheepishly. I laughed and kissed her again.

"I wouldn't want anyone else, even if you snored the whole way."

She gasped and lightly smacked my chest, "I do not snore!"

Winking at her was my only response. In reality, she didn't snore, but she did make a little sound I could best describe as purring. It was adorable and made me love her even more.

*Love.*

I was bursting with the emotion and amazed that I didn't feel the slightest bit of fear. Loving Bailey was easy, but I wasn't ready to tell her until I knew she was as lost to it as I was.

She told me what she wanted to eat and went to the bathroom to get ready for bed while I put in our room service order.

Every night she would put on her sexy little t-shirt and sleep shorts and every night, I took them off of her. I couldn't understand why she didn't cut out the middle man.

I barely tasted my food, too busy devouring my woman with my eyes and salivating over dessert. She was so sexually charged lately, it didn't take much to set her off.  Her nipples were tight, poking through her thin top and I knew she would already be wet and dripping for me. Fitting, since I was hard and leaking steady drops of pre-come.

At long last, she swallowed the last bite of her meal and I stood from the table so fast, my chair went flying backwards. I stalked over to her and pulled her up, dragging her to the bed and helping her climb on. I stripped to my boxers and came down over her body, each of us groaning as I made full contact. I dove in for a deep kiss, sucking her bottom lip into my mouth and letting it drag through my teeth. Then sweeping my tongue inside to mate with hers.

Our mouths separated and she whimpered, "I need you, Wyatt. Now."

"You want my tongue in your sweet, juicy pussy, baby? Or my cock buried deep, deep inside you?" I growled, craving her taste as much as the feel of her pussy squeezing the fuck out of my dick.

Her blue eyes were hazy with lust. "Yes," she gasped.

I chuckled, "My greedy girl. I'll give you both on one condition."

Bailey squirmed underneath me, her face a mask of frantic want. "What?" she cried out her question as I rocked my steel erection into her core.

"Marry me, baby," I demanded.

Apparently, she wasn't as far gone as I'd hoped because she shook her head in denial. "Wyatt, I'm not going to marry you just because I'm pregnant."

Obviously, I needed to work a little harder to convince her that while the baby was helpful in my desire to move things along quickly, we would have ended up man and wife no matter what.

The moment I saw her, she was mine and I was hers.

# Chapter 9

## Bailey

My voice didn't waiver, but my heart did. It was getting more and more difficult to tell him no each time he asked. Being tangled up with him together in bed like this made me feel so connected to him. He kissed my cheek before he licked between my lips, nipping at them. When I gasped, his tongue swept inside and all thoughts about why he kept proposing fled.

"Please, Wyatt. I need you now," I begged, the combination of Wyatt's hard, naked body over mine and the pregnancy hormones was lethal to my libido.

"Fuck," he groaned as he slid his cock inside me. I was dripping wet, and it made it easy for him to go deep. I gripped his shoulders and held on tight while he pounded into me.

"Harder," I moaned.

I rotated my hips in full circles with each downward thrust of his. After about a dozen strokes, he gripped my hips and changed the angle of his cock until he found a spot that drove me even wilder. He hammered into me, hitting the same place over and over again, pushing me to the edge. One hand slipped around my hip and slid down my belly, his thumb finding my clit and rubbing in circles. The added stimulation made me see stars as I clenched around him while I came.

My body trembled as he rode me through my climax. When I was done, he flipped me onto my stomach, pulling my knees up until I was crouched in front of him. I felt him shift into place behind me and then thrust back inside.

"Wyatt!" I gasped, clawing at the sheets as he slid in and out of me with slow, teasing strokes.

"Feels so fucking good, baby," he groaned.

"It always does." I pushed back, trying to speed up his pace, already feeling another climax building.

His hands tightened on my hips, holding me in place so I couldn't push back onto him. "Not so quick, baby. I want to take my time. Your tight, wet pussy always makes me come too fast, but not this time."

Now there was a challenge if I ever heard one. I liked knowing I made him lose control. He certainly did the same to me. "Need you to come for me," I moaned as I tried to thrust my hips behind me to force him deeper inside.

"Not until I feel you clenching around me again."

It wouldn't take much for me to go off again, and I didn't want to wait if that's what it was going to take to bring him with me. I reached down my body to flick my clit.

"Fuck, baby. Are you touching yourself?" He pounded into me harder. "That's so hot."

As I tugged at my clit, I came around his cock. Then he wrapped an arm around me and lifted me up until my back rested against his chest as he bent back, sitting on his heels. He thrust in and out, my pussy clamped on him as I bounced up and down on his lap. He pumped up into me like crazy, and I dug my nails into his thighs, along for the wild ride.

"Yes," I hissed when he thrust up one last time and held still, emptying inside of me while my orgasm crashed over my body.

Wyatt lowered me back onto the mattress, so I was resting on my stomach. "Don't you feel it, baby?"

"Feel what?" I gasped when he swiveled his hips one last time before pulling out.

"How we were made for each other," he answered, rolling onto his side and taking me with him.

I rested my head against his chest. "We certainly fit together well."

His eyes turned pensive as he gazed down at me. "I'm being serious, Bailey. I felt it from the first time I heard your laugh while sitting next to you at the bar at Jumpin' Jacks. I knew you were mine when I sunk my cock into you and found out I was your first." His hand drifted between us and settled on my belly. "I didn't even feel a moment of concern when I realized the condom broke because I knew I would marry you at some point. For weeks, I put my life on hold and searched for you because I knew there wasn't another woman in the world who I wanted for my wife but you."

"Let's do it," I heard myself say. I hadn't even known the words were in my head, let alone were going to pop out of my mouth. I clapped my hands over my lips in surprise, my eyes widening in wonder when I realized the ramification of what I'd just said and how much I really meant it. The only thing which had been holding me back from saying yes each time Wyatt had asked me to marry him before was my certainty that he was only asking because of the baby. But hearing him now, I finally understood how wrong I'd been. As impossible as it was to believe, Wyatt wanted me. Just me, baby or no baby. And I wanted him, too.

"Do what, baby?"

I sat up, turning on my knees to stare down at him. "Let's get married. Now, before heading back home." His abdominal muscles tightened underneath my palm as he bent upwards. I hurried to explain, afraid he wouldn't agree with my idea. "We aren't far from Vegas, right? Let's hop back in the car and find a chapel and get married. Tonight."

"You want to get married tonight?" he repeated, a huge grin spreading across his face.

"Yeah," I sighed. "I really do."

"Hell yes!" he roared, jumping from the bed and lifting me up to twirl me around. Then he gently placed me back on my feet. He threw his clothes back on before helping me with mine. "I know I should insist you get some sleep and getting married can wait until the morning, but I promised myself I'd get my ring on your finger as soon as I possibly could and I'm not about to waste a single moment now that you've said yes."

My eyes filled with tears as I watched him toss all our stuff back into our bags. "Won't we need all that stuff when we come back after?"

He zipped the bags up and flung them over his shoulder. "We aren't coming back, baby. We might be about to do the whole Vegas wedding thing, but I'm not about to spend my wedding night with my beautiful bride in a no-name hotel on the side of the road."

I glanced up at the moon while he practically dragged me to the truck. "There's not going to be much of a night left to enjoy."

He helped me into the passenger seat, buckling my belt for me and then headed to his side of the truck and hopped in, turning the key and pulling out of the parking lot. "It'll be more than enough since it's the first night you'll have my ring on your finger and my last name as your own."

"Rings," I gasped, my eyes tearing up again when I realized how unprepared I was for a wedding. "And a dress. Flowers."

Wyatt stretched his arm out, lacing his fingers through mine and squeezing tightly. "I've already got the ring covered, baby. I've been carrying it around with me for weeks."

If he'd really bought a ring weeks ago, there was something I didn't understand. "You never showed me a ring when you asked me to marry you."

"Would it have made a difference?"

I thought about it for a moment. "Yeah, it might have."

"Well, now I know you want me for more than the diamond ring in my pocket."

I laughed lightly. "And I know you want me for more than the baby in my belly."

"It sounds like we have the biggest problem solved, then. How about you do a quick Internet search and find out which chapel is the best and make sure they offer dresses, tuxes, and flowers."

I looked him up and down, thinking of the sight of him in a tux standing at the end of the aisle waiting for me. We were less than an hour from the strip, and I could hardly wait to see if the reality was better than my imagination.

Three hours later, I discovered my fantasies didn't even come close. Wyatt stood next to the minister and I sped up my pace in my rush to get to him. As soon as I got close, he stepped forward and grasped my hands in his. "You look stunning."

I felt beautiful. The moment I'd seen the ivory lace wedding dress hanging in the racks of gowns available, I knew it was the one I had to wear. The wedding coordinator, who was now acting as our witness, had told me I'd picked one of the new dresses which had just arrived that afternoon. I'd be the first, and last, bride to wear it because Wyatt had told her to add it to his tab. Of course, I'd teased him about wanting it for when our baby girl got married someday.

"You're not too shabby yourself."

The ceremony passed by in a blur and before I knew it, we'd been declared man and wife. Before the minister was able to tell Wyatt he could kiss his bride, his lips were on mine. It was the gentlest kiss he'd given me but still filled with all the passion we felt for each other.

"You're officially mine, Mrs. Kincaid."

He went about showing me exactly how much I was his, all night long, before bundling me into the truck the next morning and letting me sleep for the rest of the drive home. Well, except for the following night in the hotel where I got very little sleep.

# Chapter 10

## WYATT

I almost couldn't believe it when I woke up the morning after our wedding, and the next, and even more so the first one where we woke together in our house. I found myself immediately reaching for Bailey's hand to make sure there was a ring on it. Now the world would know she was mine. *Mrs. Kincaid.* Damn, I loved the sound of that.

Opening my eyes and realizing that we were finally home in our bed, I breathed a sigh of contentment before I noticed that Bailey wasn't in my arms. It was surprising since she tended to sleep plastered to my body. Not that I was complaining.

I sat up, looking around. "Baby?" I felt a stirring of panic, thinking maybe she changed her mind and ran. The sound of someone getting sick reached my ears at that moment, and I felt like an idiot for my momentary freakout. I jumped up and walked swiftly to the bathroom, finding Bailey on her knees over the toilet.

Grabbing a cloth, I ran it under cool water and swiped it over her forehead before resting it on her neck. "Hey," I murmured, "are you alright?"

She sat up and glared at me, "No! I'm puking my guts out and it's all your damn fault!"

"I'm sorry, baby." I put on my best sympathetic face, I felt bad that she was sick, but I wasn't at all sorry that she was carrying my baby.

"No you're not," she practically snarled. "I can see the macho caveman in there dancing a fucking jig at the proof that he got his woman pregnant." I laughed, but quickly sobered when her eyes narrowed and the look in her eyes became violent. Scooping her up, I set her on the bathroom counter and grabbed her toothbrush, handing it over after I put toothpaste on it.

While she brushed, I turned on the shower, then returned to her side to take care of my own teeth.

"Om gon ge at," she mumbled around her toothbrush.

I rinsed, then moved to stand between her legs, the expression on her face was forlorn. I raised an eyebrow. "Want to try that again without a mouth full of foam?"

She leaned to the side, over the sink, to spit and rinse then sat back up facing me.

"I'm going to get fat." Her voice was morose and her eyes were getting watery. "You'll look like that"—she gestured to my naked body—"and I'll look like a whale."

I rubbed her little baby bump with one hand and placed the other on her cheek. "This belly is going to be swollen with our baby and I can't wait to watch it grow. You'll never be less than gorgeous to me, Bailey, and seeing your sexy little body round with my kid will only add to your beauty."

"But, I'll be bitchy and hormonal, you aren't going to want to have sex with a mean, fat lady," she whined.

I couldn't hold in the chuckle this time, which earned me a punch in the arm.

"I will always," I started and placed my palms on her shoulders, "always, want this body," I smoldered. I took my time admiring every delicious inch of her. Her large tits, her wide hips, so perfect for gripping as I thrust into her, her thick thighs that squeezed so tight, and her pink, succulent pussy. I slid my hands down her arms, then moved them back up to rest on her collarbone before watching them descend to cup her full tits.

Her nipples hardened and I gently squeezed them, earning a low moan from her. "These are already mouthwatering and they are getting bigger. How could I not crave them?" Continuing the journey down, I grasped her hips and yanked her up against me, forcing her to circle my waist with her legs or lose her balance.

Her naked pussy was snug up against my cock. He was already standing at morning attention, but the heat and slick moisture of her core had him hardening to the point of pain.

She moaned again and I nipped at her lips, rocking into her slowly. "I could never stop wanting this pussy clamping down on my cock and "—I dragged a finger through her wet folds, then brought the finger to my lips and licked it clean—"eating this pussy will always be my favorite meal."

Bailey surged forward and fused our lips together, just as I drove into her soaked pussy. We both cried out, our sounds of passion swallowed in each other's mouths.

Kissing down the column of her throat, I licked and sucked until I reached one taut little peak and wrapped my lips around it. I loved the sounds she made when we were fucking. It only fueled my need for her and I sucked her nipple deep into my mouth to hear her cry out my name.

Letting it go with a little pop, I purred, "And I'll make damn fucking sure that you will always want me, need me too."

"I do, Wyatt," she groaned as I licked and sucked on her other tit, not wanting it to feel left out. "I need you."

"You sure as fuck do," I grunted, picking up speed as I thrust into her tight pussy. Her legs were shaking and the walls of her pussy were gripping my dick. She was getting close.

"You're hot as fuck, baby. You know that? I'll never get enough of the way you glove my cock, so fucking tight. Hold on," I warned. Moving my hands to her ass, I lifted her off of the counter and her legs tightened, her hands flying to my shoulders as I pushed her back up against the wall, so she was high enough that I could change the angle, thrusting up into her and hitting that sweet spot every time.

"Oh, Wyatt!" She yelled, "Harder!"

"You want it harder, baby?" I crooned. "Then I want to hear you scream."

Her head was back, exposing her neck and I licked a path up to her mouth, biting down on her bottom lip before mating our mouths. Slamming my cock into her hot, juicy pussy, I could feel a tingle starting in my spine and my balls drawing up tight.

"Come on, baby," I encouraged.

"Wyatt!" She screamed as she splintered in my arms, her voice ringing in my ears, setting off my own orgasm.

"Bailey! Fuck!" I shouted, coming so hard I saw stars.

I lazily pumped in and out until we were both calmed from the storm, and then carried her into the shower, still inside her. She wiggled when she felt the hot spray of the water and as if on cue, my cock hardened all over again.

I fucked her again, sitting on the bench in the steamy, glass space. Then we washed each other, taking even longer to finish when I couldn't help making her come one more time on my tongue. To my exquisite pleasure, she returned the gesture.

Finally dressed and ready for the day, I was making Bailey breakfast when her phone started to ring. "Baby," I called, "phone."

She rushed into the room, her tiny shorts were hugging her ass and her tank hugging her generous tits, the front dipping, showing a little too much cleavage. There was no way in hell she would be leaving the house like that.

"Jack!" she exclaimed as she answered.

I winked and enjoyed the pink tint to her cheeks before I turned back to cooking, leaving her to her conversation.

"Sure," I could hear the smile in her voice and felt a matching one steal across my face.

"Um, let me ask Wyatt...because he's my—um..." Her voice dropped, but I still picked up on her furious whisper. "No, I can't come without him...we're together."

She was getting distressed, so I decided to address why she hadn't told him I was her husband. Later. I was more focused on why the fuck Jack was upsetting my wife.

I walked over and put my hand out, silently asking for the phone. She shook her head and brought the phone to her chest. "Jack and my dad want to have dinner tonight," she said hesitantly.

I narrowed my eyes, not happy with the suggestion, but the pleading look on her face had me nodding with an unhappy sigh. I swear, if Jack caused her any more pain, I was going to beat the living daylights out of the jackass.

"Ok, we'll be there at six." She hung up the phone and put it on the counter, then walked over and put her arms around me, resting her head on my back. "Thank you."

I placed my hands over hers where they were clasped on my chest. "You don't have to thank me, baby. They're your family, too." Breaking her hold, I rotated around until I was facing her, cupping her face in my hands. "But, I'm warning you, if Jack doesn't back the fuck off, we're leaving until he gets his head out of his ass."

Bailey gave me a small smile and a micro-chuckle, kissed me, and sat at the bar while I plated our breakfast and brought it over.

"Baby."

"Hmmm?"

"You want to tell me why you neglected to tell your brother that we got married?"

She practically stuffed her face full of food, so she couldn't answer and shrugged, not meeting my eyes.

"Bailey," I admonished.

She swallowed slowly, but I waited her out.

"I wanted to tell them all together, at once."

I watched her for a few minutes as we ate, my brows furrowed in suspicion. "You're sure that's all it was?"

She sighed. "Yes, Wyatt. Now, what's the plan for today?" she asked, deftly changing the subject and I decided to let her get away with it.

"We should get you unpacked."

"It's just a couple of boxes, it shouldn't take long." She shrugged and pushed her empty plate away.

I grabbed up the dishes and busied myself at the sink as I casually answered, "It's all of your stuff, baby. We need to unload it and find a place for everything."

"What do you mean, 'it's all my stuff'?"

I heard her footsteps as she ran outside to look in the truck and subsequently heard her bellowing my name.

It took half an hour of being called bossy, domineering, and controlling (I decided it was definitely a bad idea to remind her that those were all the same thing. I might just have a bruise from where she punched me in the chest) for me to calm her down and remind her that married people lived together, so none of her shit should be at her *old* house.

We spent the day moving her in. Well, I moved things and refused to let her help, much to her annoyance, saying only, "Baby," with a pointed look at her stomach, to get her to back down.

We got ready and headed to her dad's house a little before six. When we arrived, Milo and Sharon greeted us at the door, sweeping Bailey up into a hug. I tugged her back into my arms after a few moments, jealous of anyone else's arms being around her, even her dad and step mom.

Sharon suddenly squealed and grabbed Bailey's hand, yanking her out of my grasp again. I grumbled, but reluctantly let her go to show off the rings that announced she now belonged to me.

"It's gorgeous, Bailey!" Sharon sent a dirty look my way when she caught sight of the wedding band resting next to the diamond engagement ring. "Although, it would have been nice to be at our only daughter's wedding and have her father walk her down the aisle."

Milo laughed and clapped me on the back. "I should have known when you said you were driving through Vegas. Just couldn't wait, huh?"

I looked him in the eye and said, "No, sir." I wasn't going to apologize for making Bailey mine officially, the moment she said yes. Never mind that it was Bailey's idea to get married right away.

Sharon huffed, "We'll just have to plan a proper wedding, and it doesn't matter if you're already married."

Milo shook my hand and winked. "Welcome to the family, son. Treat her right or I'll bury you where no one will ever find you."

I stifled a chuckle, "Yes, sir."

We all stepped inside and moved toward the couches, Sharon chatting happily about all of her wedding plans. Bailey threw me an amused glance and shrugged.

"Oh! Milo!" Sharon exclaimed, "Get the champagne, we need to celebrate and toast the new husband and wife."

She turned to Bailey, beaming, "Well not you—"

"What the fuck?!" Jack's outraged shout stopped Sharon cold and we all looked to see him standing just inside the door. His eyes were pointed directly at me, rage darkening his blue eyes to almost black.

"You talked her into a quickie wedding?" he seethed, his voice shifting to a deadly calm.

"Jack—" Bailey stood and took a step towards him, but I grabbed her arm and pulled her into my side, cutting her off.

"We made the decision together, Jack," I grit out between my teeth. "We are having a baby and want to be a family."

"We're her family," Jack thumped himself on the chest, over his heart. "You don't even know her. If you did, then you would have given my baby sister the wedding she deserved instead of a sham Vegas wedding without any of us there."

His gaze dropped and he looked at Bailey, his face softening. "I'm here for you, little sister. You didn't have to rush anything. I will be here for you to lean on if you want to change your mind. Maybe get to know—"

I'd had enough. "Jack!" I shouted, "She is my *wife*. You need to back the fuck off and accept it."

"Jack, this was my decision and I need to see if I can make this work. If it doesn't, you'll be the first one I'll call."

"If it doesn't work?" There is no disguising the hurt and anger from my voice.

Bailey put her hand on my arm, drawing my attention, "Calm down, Wyatt. We just found each other and haven't had much time as a family. He's afraid you'll take me away again and he won't be there to protect me."

"Protect you from what?"

"From me getting hurt."

I staggered back a little. "You think I could ever hurt you?"

"Of course you can hurt her. You don't know the first thing about commitment, Wyatt," Jack piped up, and I shot metal daggers at him through my eyes.

Bailey growled in frustration, "Would you two knock it the fuck off?"

Then she sighed and rubbed her stomach, looking at me. "You don't really know me, Wyatt, and I don't know you all that well either. I'm just trying to say that I can understand why he's worried things won't work out."

I shook my head a little, confused and hurt. "It was your idea to get married in Vegas. If you thought this wouldn't last, why would you agree to marry me?"

"I do think this will—" Bailey gasped and bent over slightly, her hands cradling her belly. She looked up at me with pain written on her face and tears starting to roll down her cheeks. I grabbed her arms in a panic, not understanding what was happening. With another gasp, she suddenly curled into herself, hugging her middle tight. Her face drained of color, her eyes closed, and I caught her right before her head hit the ground.

# Chapter 11

## Bailey

"I'm scared," I cried, my hold on Wyatt's hand tightening while I waited on a bed in the emergency room. We'd been here for several hours already, and they'd run numerous tests to see what was going on. The pain was gone, leaving only light cramping in its wake, but the blood stain I'd found in the gusset of my panties when I changed into the hospital gown they'd given me was what had me completely freaked out.

"I'm here, baby." His thumb rubbed the underside of my wedding ring, a reminder that we were in this together as man and wife. "No matter what."

I was barely holding on by a thread, the feel of his hand on mine the only thing keeping me sane. Jack kept hold of my other hand. He hadn't said a word since we arrived and he'd insisted he was coming back with us. My dad and Sharon were in the waiting room, and I knew the only reason none of us had argued with my brother was because we all knew he felt guilty for starting the argument with Wyatt.

"I'm sorry," I whispered, staring up at my Wyatt with tears running down my cheeks.

"You don't have anything to be sorry about," he reassured me.

But I did. I felt horrible for hurting him earlier. For not being able to find the right words. I'd only been trying to talk my brother down from his anger, to make him see that I knew he had my back, even though Wyatt was his best friend. "What I was saying before? When the pain started? I was trying to tell you I *do* think this will last. I would never have suggested we get married right away if I didn't."

"Baby," he sighed, his gaze moving to Jack before coming back to me. "Don't worry about that right now. It isn't important."

"It is," I insisted. "You need to know how happy I was to become your wife."

"Seriously, Bailey," he growled. "This is the last thing you need to be focused on right now."

"Wyatt's right, little sis," Jack agreed.

It was nice to hear my brother backing up his best friend after all the arguing. "It kills me to know I'm the reason you're fighting."

"We're done with the fighting," Wyatt declared.

"You are?" My gaze darted between the two of them.

"We are," Jack confirmed, smiling at me before shifting his focus on Wyatt. "I've been a dick and I'm sorry."

"No apologies needed, man. I get it. She's your sister and you want what's best for her. I can respect that."

"I do want what's best for her," Jack agreed. "And if I hadn't been so damn busy freaking out at the idea of losing my baby sister to my best friend, I would have admitted she couldn't do any better than you."

"Shit, Jack. You've got to know I'll do whatever it takes to make her happy."

"I know you will," my brother smiled down at me. "I've seen it for myself with how you've been taking care of her ever since we got here."

And my thoughts went back to why we were in the hospital in the first place. "What if there's something wrong with the pregnancy?"

"I'll never forgive myself," Jack muttered. "I should have pulled my head out of my ass before I managed to land you in the emergency room."

"I'm the one who was arguing with her," Wyatt pointed out.

"It's not your fault. Either of you."

"You should listen to my patient. She's right," a doctor we hadn't seen before told the guys as she walked into the exam room. Her eyes slid to my hands, her brow quirking up when she noted both men were holding one. "Mrs. Kincaid, would you prefer to be alone while we talk?"

"I'm not going anywhere," Wyatt growled, glaring at the doctor.

"Neither am I," Jack added.

"My husband and brother are anxious about me," I explained, "and the baby."

Her stance relaxed as she sat down on a stool and rolled it towards my bed. "I'm Dr. Harris, one of the OBGYNs with privileges here at the hospital. I bumped into your emergency room physician and he asked if I'd take a look at your chart, come in, and speak with you."

"Okay," I whispered, tensing up because this didn't sound good.

"It's not a bad thing," she assured me. "Since your husband mentioned to him that you hadn't found a doctor of your own yet because you wanted a female, he thought you might like to meet me as long as we were both here."

"Oh!" I gasped, understanding dawning and relief setting in. If the emergency room doctor thought I needed an OBGYN then—"I'm not miscarrying?"

"None of the tests indicate a miscarriage," she confirmed.

"Thank goodness," I breathed.

"What about the pain?"

"Why did she faint?"

Wyatt and Jack asked their questions in unison.

"How's the pain now?" the doctor asked, her gaze on the tablet in her hands. "You described it as a four on a scale of one to ten when you first arrived. Is it still at the same level?"

"No," I whispered. "I'd say it's more like a two right now. I'd describe it as cramping instead of pain."

"That's great to hear," she murmured, looking up at me and smiling. "Cramping during the early stage of pregnancy is normal unless it's accompanied by severe pain or bleeding."

"There was blood in my panties when I took them off," I whispered.

"Spotting can be normal, too. As long as it wasn't full flow then it was nothing to be concerned about."

"And the fainting?" I asked.

"Well, your blood sugar is a little low which could explain why you fainted," she replied. "When's the last time you ate today?"

"She barely touched her breakfast and only had a light lunch," Wyatt answered for me.

"We were meeting for dinner at our dad's house when she fainted," Jack added.

"I've been having problems with morning sickness," I defended. "It's more like all day sickness."

"I'll write you a prescription for some anti-nausea meds which are safe for the baby," the doctor offered. "I'll see if they have any of the ginger pops my patients rave about so you can take a few home with you and see if they work for you. Then I'd like for you to call my office to schedule an appointment this week to follow-up and discuss the plan for your pregnancy going forward."

"That's it?" I asked.

"Yup," she confirmed. "Call my office if the spotting or cramps get worse before your appointment. And from what I heard when I walked in, I'd also advise you to avoid heated arguments as much as possible. You don't need the added stress during your pregnancy."

"No more arguing," Wyatt promised, squeezing my hand.

"Or stress of any kind," my brother added.

"If you figure out how to manage that, let me know," the doctor laughed, getting back to her feet. "A nurse will be in soon to go over your discharge paperwork and then you can head home."

"I'll go give Dad and Sharon the good news." Jack dropped a kiss on my forehead before following her out the door.

"Love you, Bailey," Wyatt murmured.

"Love you, too."

His free hand moved to rest on my belly. "You and my baby boy."

"Baby girl," I corrected lightly, relieved to know he or she was safe and sound and we could get back to teasing each other about the pregnancy.

As promised, the nurse came in to discharge me—and walked in on us sharing a passionate kiss. A few minutes later, I was being rolled out to the waiting room in a wheelchair by Wyatt, who'd refused to let anyone else push me.

"Are you two knuckleheads done being stupid?" my dad asked, he and Sharon both jumping to their feet as soon as they saw us. The power of his glare was lessened by the sight of him holding a giant stuffed teddy bear, though.

"Yeah, we're done," Wyatt confirmed.

Jack nodded in agreement. "It's a good thing, too, because I think Wyatt's going to need all the help he can get keeping my sister in line."

"Oh, crap," I groaned at the thought of the two of them ganging up on me for the rest of my pregnancy.

"I'm pretty sure I can handle her," Wyatt chuckled.

The shiver that went down my spine at the sound of his laughter confirmed he could handle me. He'd been able to since the moment we met, after all. I didn't expect it to change anytime soon, if ever.

# *Epilogue*

## WYATT

"Let's see here." Dr. Harris moved the ultrasound wand around, clicking here and there with the mouse. I waited impatiently, my weight shifting from foot to foot until Bailey let go of my hand to run a soothing palm down my arm before lacing our fingers together again.

"Relax, Wyatt," she said, clearly suppressing a laugh.

I tore my eyes from the black and white screen and drank in the sight of my beautiful wife. She was glowing with excitement, as anxious as I was, but not nearly as nervous. I bent down and kissed her softly, resting my forehead on hers for a moment before we both turned our attention back to the monitor.

Listening to the rhythmic thumping of two heart beats, I still couldn't believe we were having twins. After the scare early in her pregnancy, she was checked a little more often. At about ten weeks, the doctor informed us that the ultrasound revealed two babies. Bailey was over the moon, and don't get me wrong, I was ecstatic. I swelled with pride that my boys managed to knock up my woman with two babies in one shot. But, I was also terrified. What if we had two girls? How would I protect them both from boys at the same time? I started researching all girl schools and making a list: pepper spray—no, a Taser, there had to be some kind of modern day chastity belt I could get, karate lessons—

"You definitely want to know the sex of the babies, Mr. and Mrs. Kincaid?" The doctor's question interrupted my thoughts.

Bailey squeezed my hand and nodded, but still answered out loud, "Absolutely."

"Congratulations, it looks life two girls." Dr. Harris smiled and faced the monitor again.

"Shit," I whispered, "I am so totally fucked."

Bailey smacked my arm, she'd been after me to start watching my language.

I couldn't imagine how shell shocked I must've looked as I stood there muttering, "Shotgun, I need a fucking shotgun. And a Taser gun—

Once again my thoughts were interrupted, this time by Bailey's giggling. Dr. Harris threw me an amused glance and Bailey's hands were clamped over her mouth, but she couldn't contain her laughter. I glared at her, "Baby, there is nothing funny about this"—my eyes narrowed—"and don't be thinking I've forgotten about that spanking," I growled.

Her eyes heated, obviously not opposed to the idea and I had to adjust myself in hopes of hiding my growing erection.

"Oh, wait," the doctor said. Our heads whipped in her direction simultaneously. Was something wrong with my baby girls?

She must have noticed the lack of color in our faces because she quickly reassured us that they were healthy and everything was normal.

"Baby number two was hiding his little penis."

I perked up immediately, "His? His penis?" I clarified.

"Yes," she confirmed, pointing to the little thing between my baby's legs.

I sighed, utterly relieved, "She'll have a brother to help me protect her."

*Seven Years Later*

"Mommy!" Julia yelled, her voice indignant. "Peter tried to share his snack with me on the playground and Jack chased him away!"

I smiled as my sweet girl stomped into the kitchen, her cute little face screwed up in anger. "Hey, Marshmallow," I greeted, scooping her up and nuzzling her nose with mine, then I kissed the tip. She giggled, "I'm Snickers today, daddy." I laughed as I put her back down, we playfully argued over which "sweet" she was every day.

Back on her feet, Julia's petite fists went to her hips and she glared at Jack as he entered the room. "Now he won't want to be my boyfriend," she snapped. Jack's little chest puffed up with pride and I held out my fist. He bumped it with a wide smile. "That's my boy."

"Wyatt!" Bailey scolded in warning as she walked into the room. I shrugged, not a bit sorry that I'd taught my son how to be a big brother. She rolled her eyes and corralled both kids towards the bathroom to help them wash up for dinner. She was talking to Jack about leaving Julia's friends alone when he glanced back at me and I winked. He smiled broadly but quickly dropped it when Bailey glared at both of us.

I finished setting the table and went to check on my other precious baby girl. Four-year-old Hayley was coloring in her room and gave me a big grin when I stepped inside.

"Want to cowor wif me, Daddy?"

Any time either of my girls called me daddy, my chest warmed all over and I would give them just about anything they wanted. They had me wrapped around their little fingers.

"After dinner, Hayley bug." I lifted her into my arms and she slipped her small arms around my neck and squeezed me tight. I melted a little and thought, damn, I had a great life.

"That's it, baby, take me deep," I growled as I pushed into my wife's pussy from behind. I was getting even harder watching my dick disappear under her perfectly round ass. I gripped her generous hips, fuck, I loved those hips, and pulled her back to meet each thrust.

"Wyatt!" she cried out and I grunted with satisfaction at hearing her loud and lusty voice. The kids were with my parents and we had the house to ourselves for a night. I intended to take advantage and have her screaming all night long.

"Let me hear you, baby. Fuck, I miss hearing how loud you are when I fuck you."

Bailey moaned and shifted for a better angle, careful of her large stomach. I slowed my thrusts to a maddeningly lazy speed, smiling at her growl of frustration. My hands glided around to hold her swollen belly. Leaning over her, I whispered, "You know you're in trouble, right baby?" I asked, my voice husky and thick with desire.

"Yes," she groaned. We'd been to the doctor that day and found out we were having another beautiful little girl. Jack and I would be outnumbered and I was very clear when she got pregnant again that it had better be a boy. My girls were too gorgeous and needed extra protection.

I lifted one hand and the next time I pushed inside, I brought it down, leaving a pink handprint on her creamy white skin, jiggling from the spanking. She shuddered and shoved back against me, trying to entice me to speed up.

I wanted to tease and torment her, but I didn't have enough control. I picked up speed again, returning to her hips and gripping so tight, she'd probably have bruises in the morning. I spanked her again and she screamed in pleasure as her body started to shake, her orgasm approaching.

"Hold on, baby," I commanded. "Not yet. I want to feel your pussy sucking me in a little longer."

She clenched her walls and I shouted," Fuck!"

I slapped her ass again. The little minx was trying to make me lose control. But, all that did was build my own frenzy and I pummeled into her, heat shooting straight to my balls. "Oh fuck, baby," I hissed when she clenched again. "That feels so damn good. I'll never stop craving your sexy body. I'm addicted to fucking you."

"Wyatt," she moaned, "I need you too."

"In fact," her voice became a little irritated, "I need you right now!" she demanded.

I laughed at my greedy girl and gave her what she wanted, not having the ability to keep from giving her anything she asked for.

My fingers found her clit and I pinched it hard. Her screams set me off and I exploded inside her.

Our breathing had only just evened out when we went for another round, this time unhurried. We enjoyed our rare moments when we didn't have to rush in case the kids woke up. I explored and worshiped every inch of her incredible body, making love to her, and when I came, I gave my heart over to her. Like I did every time I was inside her, every time she smiled, every time I looked at her and remembered she was mine.

I gathered her up, spooning her, my hand gently rubbing circles over the life we'd created. Fuck, this woman was so perfect and she belonged to me. I adored her and our babies, loved them with all of my being. And, I was probably handing over my man card for saying this, but every day, I was grateful for the shitty manufacturing of a condom.

# *Bonus Scene: Theme Park*

## WYATT

"Dad! Can you stop making out with Mom in public? It's gross!" Julia's face was screwed up in disgust, and I couldn't help but laugh.

"Julia, you're twelve years old. You should be used to it by now," I quipped with a wink.

She made another face and spun on her heel, stomping off. Jack followed after her, but not before throwing us his own look of irritation.

"Not too far, you two!" Bailey yelled.

She sat down on a bench and started what looked like a very intense (what could be so intense about a twelve-year-old's life, I have no clue) conversation and ignoring us. After a few minutes of pouting, she was giggling, her twin making her smile, the incident clearly forgotten. Laughing, I wrapped my arms around my wife and we watched our other girls on the merry-go-round, waving to them each time it made a complete rotation.

We'd decided to take our kids to Disney World for their spring break. When we surprised them with the trip, Jack and Julia had informed us that they were too old for amusement parks. Bailey and I had rolled our eyes and told them we'd be taking them to Universal. Suddenly, they were all smiles and eager to go. It had been my wife's idea because the twins were obsessed with the movies, and she turned to me with a smug smile, "Know your audience, Wyatt."

I tilted my head down and brushed my lips over the sensitive skin behind Bailey's ear, enjoying the shiver that raced down her spine. It was a good thing she was standing in front of me, because those little shivers never failed to turn me on. Fourteen years together, and my wife was still as gorgeous as the day I met her.

"Baby, you better have scheduled some sexy time in our itinerary," I whispered sternly. "Or you're going to find yourself in the nearest dark corner with a red ass once the kids are asleep." We'd been in Florida for five days, and I was like a man in the desert with no water. I loved my little cock blockers more than life, but fuck, I was desperate to be buried deep inside my wife's pussy.

Bailey shifted and I swear she rubbed up against my cock on purpose, the tease. "Patience is a virtue," she tisked. I growled and opened my mouth to retort when I felt a tap on my shoulder. Turning, I saw Milo and Sharon standing there with snide smiles on their faces.

The ride came to a halt and happy shrieks of "Grandma! Grandpa!" sounded as two pairs of little feet came running over to them, their parents all but forgotten.

Perfect timing. "Hey. Give your mom and me some sugar. You're going to hang with Grandma and Grandpa for—" I broke off and looked to Bailey.

"Three days." Halle-fucking-lujah, my wife was amazing. We hadn't had some time away, just the two of us, in years. We hugged our little ones, then I grabbed Bailey's hand and dragged her over to Julia and Jack. I pulled them up from their seat, one at a time, and gave them a hug, not letting go of Bailey's hand while she did the same. "See you in a few days, Cotton Candy," I said to Julia as I kissed her forehead.

"Where are you guys going?" she called out as I began to drag Bailey away.

"To make out in private!" I yelled back, then bent and grabbed my wife around the waist and threw her over my shoulder, fireman style. I stalked to the park entrance in record time with Bailey half-heartedly protesting through her laughter.

# Baby Steps

Yeah, Baby 2

FIONA DAVENPORT

# Chapter 1

## Jade

"I'm sure your step-brother will be here shortly."

"Step-brother?" I repeated dumbly, having no clue what the heck the lawyer was talking about. When I got the call yesterday, I thought the request to come to Mr. Wilkinson's office to discuss my mom's death was odd. She had died four weeks ago and I wasn't expecting to inherit anything from her since she didn't have much to pass down to me except maybe some debts. Although, when I attempted to take care of them, they'd been mysteriously paid off. Then, when I'd entered their posh offices and been ushered in to see one of the named partners without waiting, I'd wondered if they'd mistaken me for someone else. Now, the mention of a mystery step-brother cinched it. I knew for sure something weird was going on here. "There must be a mistake. I don't have a step-brother."

He rifled through a stack of papers on his desk and pulled one out. "Your mom was Diamond Jones, correct?"

I cringed at his use of her full first name. She hated it and preferred to be called Di, which was odd when you thought about it since she named me after a gem too. *What kind of person who hated being named after a precious jewel turned around and named their only child after one?* It made no sense to me. Then again, I never claimed to understand anything about my mom. She and I had always been polar opposites. "Yes."

He stretched his arm across the desk and handed the paper to me. I glanced down and the words "Marriage Certificate" jumped out at me. My mom was listed as the bride, and it was dated for the day before the car crash which took her life four weeks ago. "My mom got married?"

Sympathy shone from the lawyer's eyes. "Theirs was a whirlwind courtship. I'm sure she was going to discuss it with you when she and Jonathan returned from their honeymoon. He was a very private man, and there were public relations issues to work out before they went public with the marriage."

My mom married a guy who had to take public relations issues into consideration? One whose fancy lawyer referred to him by his first name? *Oh, Mama. You finally landed the golden goose you'd always dreamed of, only to die the next day. If that wasn't irony biting you in the ass, I didn't know what was.*

"When I was contacted about her death, the police mentioned there was a man in the car with her at the time. Was it Jonathan? Did he survive the crash?"

"I'm sorry to say he lingered in the hospital for a week before passing away," he explained. "Unfortunately, someone dropped the ball and neglected to contact you sooner so we could help with the arrangements for her funeral and make sure you were taken care of during this time of crisis."

"Thank you," I whispered. "But I have everything under control. My mom has already been buried. I spoke with her landlord and the rent on her apartment was already paid up for last month and this one too. I have a little time before I need to clear it out which was a godsend since I have a show to prepare for and not a lot of free time right now."

"I don't think you'll find many personal effects at the apartment. I believe most of her things had already been moved into Jonathan's estate," he explained. "If you need additional time, I'm sure we can make arrangements to have the remainder of her items packed up and moved for you."

"That's kind of you to offer, but I guess I don't really understand what I'm doing here."

"My assistant should have explained when she called yesterday." He sent an irritated glance towards his door, as though she could see him. "You've been named in Jonathan's will."

"Why would he even do that when we'd never met? I mean, I didn't even know he existed," I mumbled the last part, cringing a little at blurting it out like that. "When would he have had time to add me to his will?"

"Jonathan was a man who knew how to get things done quickly." I held back an inappropriate giggle while thinking about how fast my mom had to have moved to get him to marry her so swiftly. Apparently spritzing men's cologne in a high-end department store finally paid off. "And considering the size of his estate, he didn't want to leave anything to chance once your mom was a part of his life."

I couldn't help but think of all the men who'd paraded through my mom's world while I was growing up. As different as we were and despite the distance between us, I loved her dearly. It was deeply saddening to know she'd finally met a man who apparently treasured her the way she'd always wanted, only to die shortly afterward.

I stood, intending to step away for a moment to gain control of my emotions before I ended up sobbing in front of a stranger. My stomach had another form of embarrassment in mind instead. The breakfast burrito I'd gobbled down this morning crept back up my throat. My gaze darted around the room, frantically searching for a place where I could vomit. "I think I'm going to be sick," I mumbled past the hand I'd slapped over my mouth.

The lawyer rolled his chair back and started to pull a trash can out from under his desk. I didn't have enough time to wait for him and scampered around to his side, falling to my knees and thanking my lucky stars when my puke hit the bottom of the trash can. A couple minutes later, once my stomach was empty, I realized I'd trapped Mr. Wilkinson in his chair because the wall was right behind him. Grabbing the handkerchief he was holding out for me and lifting it to swipe at my lips, I felt my cheeks heat as I rose to my feet again.

"What the hell are you doing here, Jade?" The question was growled from behind me in a raspy voice with which I was intimately familiar. I swiveled on my heel and came face-to-face with Lucas St. James. In his three-piece suit, with his dark hair perfectly styled and chocolate brown eyes glaring daggers at me, he looked nothing like the man who'd left me tousled and naked in a hotel room bed six weeks ago. "And why the fuck were you giving my dad's lawyer a blow job under his desk?"

I felt the little blood which was left in my face after my puke-fest drain. I wasn't sure if it was because Lucas had just said "dad" which meant he was most likely the stepbrother in question or if it was the blow job insult.

Mr. Wilkinson jumped to his feet and threw his hands up in protest. "She was doing no such thing, Lucas. You should be ashamed of yourself for even suggesting something so untoward of this sweet young woman."

Lucas's gaze dropped to my lips, his eyes heating. If I had to hazard a guess, I'd bet that he was remembering me on my knees, doing exactly what he'd just accused me of. But to him, not the lawyer. "I've done a hell of a lot more than suggest it."

*Yeah, that's exactly what he'd been doing.* My cheeks heated in embarrassment as the lawyer looked at us questioningly. Lucas had spoken low enough that he couldn't hear what he'd said, but there was no mistaking the tension between the two of us.

"Please, why don't the both of you take a seat so we can go over the details of Jonathan's will?"

I circled his desk and dropped back down into the chair I'd been seated in earlier. Lucas moved forward, coming to stand to the side of the desk instead of taking the other seat. My gaze slid up his body, enjoying the sight of his long legs and lean torso, before coming to rest on his face. His attention was directed away from me, and I took advantage of the moment to savor the masculine beauty of his face. My fingers itched with the desire to paint him, to finally do justice to the portrait I'd started over again at least a dozen times when I should have been focused on the paintings for my first show.

Our weekend together was supposed to have only been a fling, but I'd quickly become fascinated by Lucas to the point of distraction. If I hadn't been so wrapped up in meeting a looming deadline for my show while also dealing with my mom's death, I probably would have tried to find him weeks ago to convince him that I hadn't known who he was and to see if this obsession was a two-way street.

"Why in the world would *she* need to be here to discuss the terms of *my* dad's will?" Lucas's question held a healthy dose of suspicion.

"Because the woman Jonathan married the day before the car crash was her mom, and he made arrangements for Jade to be taken care of in the case of both their deaths."

"She's the gold digger's daughter?" His eyes raked me up and down, icing over. "Yeah, that makes sense."

There went the two-way street idea. Evidently, he didn't share my feelings and wasn't interested in more than what we already had together. It stung, but it was better to know now instead of later. I probably shouldn't have found the irony of my mom's situation the least bit amusing because now karma came back to bite *me* in the ass as I stared gape-mouthed at Lucas. Not only was he the man with whom I'd had a weekend fling, but he was also responsible for the most likely explanation for my persistent nausea for these past few days. *Crapballs*, it looked like I really shouldn't have put off taking a pregnancy test and hunting him down if it was positive.

## Chapter 2

## LUCAS

There was a part of me that was devastated to find out Jade was the daughter of that ditzy, conniving, gold digger who'd bewitched my dad with her ... *assets*, to gain access to *his* assets. I'd hoped my suspicions about Jade were a product of my paranoia and I hated that they'd been confirmed by this latest development.

That part still wanted to lick, bite, and suck on every inch of her skin, especially her tits as they spilled out of my hands. It begged to sink deep inside her, make her scream my name. Fuck her until we were both too exhausted to continue. Then find a little more energy and fuck her again.

The other part of me was fucking pissed. Were they in it together? Was this some kind of mother-daughter con? My father and I had always been close. He was my hero, everything I wanted to be, strong, logical, and a brilliant businessman. I followed in his footsteps, wanting to make him proud. So, when he started dating *Diamond*, a stripper name if I ever heard one, I was shocked that he would let himself be controlled by his other head, instead of the one above his shoulders. I did my best to convince him that she was only after his money, but he wouldn't be swayed.

*"Dad, you need to use your logic and get on solid ground. Then you'll see that she is only after your money," I whisper-yelled, conscious of the fact that we were in public, having lunch at a four-star restaurant.*

*He laughed and shook his head, as though I'd said something ridiculous. What the fuck was so crazy about wanting him to see through the blonde bimbo he'd proposed to the day before?*

*"You may be right, Lucas. I don't think you are, but it's possible. However, whatever her reasons were in the beginning, I promise you they've changed. When you get to be my age"—I rolled my eyes, he was sixty but with the body and energy of a man at least ten years his junior— "you get tired of being alone and if you find a beautiful woman who makes*

*you laugh and feel loved, one that is amazing in bed"—I cringed—"you do your best to woo her. And son, trust me, I know how to get and keep a woman. Looking back, I'm the one who pursued her."*

*I scoffed, "What's keeping her from running off when she gets her greedy hands on your money?" I narrowed my eyes, scrutinizing his reactions to my questions. "Let me guess, she offered to sign a prenup but the selfless gesture was enough to convince you to marry her without one?"*

*Dad's brown eyes, ones that looked exactly like mine, lit with a sliver of irritation. If I didn't know him, hadn't seen all sides of him as his son, I would have completely missed it. He could kick anyone's ass at poker and it's one of the things that made him so successful.*

*"As a matter of fact, she did offer to sign a prenup—"*

*I cut him off with a bitter laugh. "Of course she did."*

*He leaned in, looking at me with disapproval, and I withered inside, hating that look because it meant I'd disappointed him.*

*"Are you implying that I'm suddenly stupid, going senile in my old age?" he clipped.*

*Yeah, definitely feeling like a kid being scolded for talking back.*

*He continued without a response from me, "I asked her to sign a prenup and she agreed."*

*I felt my eyes widen. I was shocked.*

*"And after, I promptly tore it up."*

Not so shocked.

*"She was completely understanding about it, not the least bit insulted either."*

Aaaaand, opinion of the gold digger restored.

I glanced at Jade in my peripheral, struck once again by her beauty and angry at myself for noticing. When you have money, it's easy to become jaded (pun intended) and assume every woman is either after your fortune or what you can do for them in bed, until they prove otherwise.

I wasn't exactly sure which category Jade fell into, but like all other women, she'd gone after me because she wanted something.

I'd gotten lucky in the physical department, inheriting my father's six foot two height and naturally muscular body. With the exception of the color, my eyes and thick lashes were from my mother, as well as the hard angles of my face, though hers were obviously more feminine.

I was a computer nerd through and through, but I was able to counter balance it by playing high school football and excelling in art history. Girls dug a guy with brains and brawn.

At sixteen, my father caught me hacking into...well, places that would get me thrown in prison for the rest of my life. Instead of punishing me, he put me to work in his company. School was beyond easy for someone with my IQ, but I never said anything because I wanted to stay in the same grade and school as my friends. I thought I was getting away with it, until he informed me that he knew, but wanted me to make my own decisions.

I stayed in high school, but I started taking college classes and with the credits from working at our solar energy company, I graduated with a masters in Electrical Engineering and one in Computer Engineering by the time I was twenty. Eight years later, I'd worked my way up to executive. My father owned the company and I was to be his successor. However, we still had a board of directors who held forty-seven percent of the vote.

They were older than me, set in their ways, which frustrated me to no end considering we were supposed to be developing cutting edge solar technology. But, it wasn't the product, it was our *image* they were more concerned about. They were conservative, and the clients they brought to the table were the same. They expected your home life to reflect your business.

I'd brought up to Dad the fact that Diamond would in no way be acceptable to the board and clients we catered to at that moment. He shrugged and told me they'd get over it. That we could overrule their decisions anyway. While true, he seemed to be ignoring the fact that if any of those guys left, they would take their golf buddies, our clients, with them and I hadn't had enough time to bring in sufficient new business to withstand the loss.

I vowed to never make his same mistakes. And yet, there I was, my moment of weakness staring me in the face, with pale skin and a sickened look on her face. I wondered for half a second if she had faked our whole weekend. It was a ridiculous notion, nobody was that good an actress, and I was very well aware of my skills in the bedroom.

The chemistry between us was crackling even now, my traitorous body coming alive at being so near her. I focused on my anger, willing my cock to back the hell off. But no, it was still every bit as strong as when we first met.

My life was centered around the company and everything else came second. I needed an outlet for my creative side, though, something that was entirely separate and only mine. I had only ever shared it with my father. I'd bought a small art gallery and took great pride in helping small, local artists share their passion. In some cases, it even became the boost their career needed.

I was at the gallery one night, around six weeks ago, and after finishing up some paperwork, I decided to wander about and check out our newest artist's talents. That's when I saw her. She was average height, the top of her head reaching my shoulders. That was the only thing ordinary about her, though. Her wavy, platinum hair was pulled back from her face, in a ponytail that screamed to be pulled while she was being fucked. The profile of her face was classically beautiful, lashes so thick and long, I was curious to see up close if they were fake.

She turned and caught me giving her the once over, but it didn't stop my eyes from continuing downward, landing on the most spectacular pair of tits I'd ever seen. They were large, almost too big for her frame, but she pulled it off and my mouth practically watered at the sight of those perfectly round globes.

She was slim, with a tiny waist, a slight flare of hips, and endless legs encased in sexy stilettos. I was suddenly imagining those legs wrapped around me, squeezing me on the outside and her pussy doing the same on the inside. I swear, I almost came in my pants like a horny teenager.

She had the body of a stripper, and a bolt of jealousy shot through me at the thought of any other man seeing her naked body. It was unexpected, but it didn't stop the growing confidence that I was going to end this night with her under me. She seemed to sense where my thoughts had gone because she blushed, making my already hard cock turn to stone. She was so fucking beautiful.

We met in the middle of the room, as though we were drawn together by our chemistry. It was a fucking movie moment, a scene from one of those ridiculous chick flicks. I was beyond aroused to see that there was nothing fake about her body.

"Lucas St. James," I introduced myself.

She smiled, almost shyly. "Jade Jones."

I took back my recent thought about nothing being fake. Her name was obviously made up, and I hoped it didn't mean she actually was a stripper. I worried about the way it would look if it got out that I'd spent time with a woman like her. However, right then and there, I decided I didn't give a fuck. I was going to have her.

"I'm going to be blunt, to save wasted time," I stated, "I desperately want you under me. Can I convince you to leave and spend the night with me?"

She hesitated, and for a moment I was terrified she was going to refuse, but then she smiled again and nodded, the sweet blush returning to her cheeks.

One night in a hotel turned into a weekend and I was starting to realize that

I would almost surely never have enough of her. Then a cold bucket of reality was thrown at me.

She'd mentioned in passing that she was an artist and I assumed it was a hobby. I casually asked what had brought her to the gallery, too busy focusing on how I wanted to have her next to care about the question.

"I've turned in a portfolio and I'm hoping they'll choose me for their next show," she chattered excitedly.

I froze as the fog of lust receded, replaced by disappointment and rage. "So, this was an attempt to up your chances? Fuck the owner so he'll be too enamored with your"—I ran my eyes down her body—"charms to pick anyone else? I've got to say, Jade," I spit her name, "even if you do take your clothes off for a living, I didn't think you were the kind of girl to sell your body."

She gasped in fake indignation, but she wasn't fooling me anymore.

"What are you talking about? I haven't done that—sold my—how could you think—?" she sputtered. "Wait, you're the owner?"

I rolled my eyes and got out of bed, starting to dress. "Drop the act, Jade. It's the St. James Gallery, for fuck's sake. There's no way you didn't know it was my gallery."

Dressed, I grabbed my keys and wallet and stormed to the door. I couldn't help glancing back and saw her sitting on the bed, her eyes wide in supposed shock, her mouth forming a little *O*. For half a heartbeat, I wondered if I was wrong and she was being genuine. But, experience had taught me better, so I walked out and slammed the door shut.

# Chapter 3

## Jade

At first glance, it appeared as though Lucas's full attention was on Mr. Wilkinson while he slit open a sealed envelope and pulled out a stack of papers. But I felt the weight of his scrutiny on me as I sipped on the glass of water I'd been given and popped a piece of gum into my mouth. The hair rose on my arms the same way it had when I felt him looking at me the night we'd met. My gaze darted up quickly, only to find him sending me a sidelong glance before I tilted my head to stare down at my hands. The brief moment of eye contact was enough to send shivers down my spine while I remembered how his eyes darkened with lust until it was virtually impossible to discern the difference between his pupils and the dark brown of his irises. How it felt to dig my nails into the taut skin of his back as he hammered into me.

*Crap!* I shook my head when the clearing of Mr. Wilkinson's throat penetrated through the sensual fog that seemed to wrap around me anytime Lucas was near. It was the same effect which had me agreeing to sleep with him within minutes of our first meeting. And it was distracting me from the important matters at hand—finding out what my mom's husband of one day had left me in his will and finding a stick to pee on at the first opportunity. Finding out if I was pregnant had moved from a niggling doubt in my mind to a screaming alert of urgency. Right after I got the lawyer to repeat what he'd just said while I was shaking off my Lucas induced daze. Because clearly it had been important based on Lucas's reaction.

"You've got to be fucking kidding me!" he roared. "There's no way in hell my father was stupid enough to do this."

"Do what?" I repeated, shifting my attention away from Lucas and back to Mr. Wilkinson. "I'm sorry, could you repeat what you said?"

"Jonathan made arrangements for you to inherit half of his personal estate in the event of his and your mother's deaths. Had she survived, she would have inherited it in your place. A smaller settlement would have been made upon you, since she would have been alive to provide assistance should you need it. All of his shares in the company will go to Lucas, of course, and the other half of the personal estate as well."

"He did?" I gasped, feeling stunned by this turn of events. I hadn't even ever met him. Why had he thought to include me in his will? And why in the world did he think my mom would have helped me if I needed it? I'd been supporting myself while trying to make it as an artist without any help from her, using the money from the life insurance policy my father had left me when he passed away four years ago.

"Don't sit there, pretending to look innocent," Lucas growled. "You had to have known what your mom was up to; convincing my dad to change his will like this."

"It was actually my doing," Mr. Wilkinson interjected. "Jonathan stopped into my office a couple days before his marriage. He said he wanted to talk to me about the prenuptial agreement he'd asked me to draw up while Di was out dress shopping. He let me know it was no longer necessary, a decision I advised him against, considering the vastness of his estate. He was adamant and I had no choice but to abide by his decision."

"That doesn't explain the change in my dad's will."

"I asked him if he wanted to make any changes to it with the upcoming nuptials. I didn't want to run the risk of having assets frozen if Di ever had reason to contest it in probate court, not with the company as part of his estate."

"And at no point during this visit did it cross your mind to ask him if he'd lost his mind?" Lucas's question was thick with sarcasm.

Mr. Wilkinson leveled him with a glare. "You and I both know your father was of sound mind and body. If making decisions based on love was grounds to overturn a will, then our legal system would be in serious trouble."

"He wasn't thinking with his heart," Lucas argued. "It was his little head making the decisions for him."

"You don't know that," I snapped, knowing darn well it was entirely possible he was right but not caring in the least. Someone had to defend my mom, as she was no longer able to do it herself.

"Enough," Mr. Wilkinson grunted. "Let me get through the rest of this and then the two of you can squabble like children without my having to listen to it."

I crossed my arms over my chest defensively, only to drop them when I noticed Lucas doing the same as we both listened intently.

"Jonathan also made arrangements for any children Lucas might have, with specified amounts for trust funds to be set aside and such."

"Not like that's going to happen any time soon."

My hand drifted to my stomach, the very place where his baby might already rest. I hoped like hell he was right and I was suffering from some strange, lingering illness instead of pregnancy. I'd take just about any kind of sickness as an explanation right about now.

"The final stipulation is that in order to inherit, you're both expected to reside in the family home for the next year."

The room was suddenly filled with absolute silence. You literally could have heard a pin drop. I must have heard him wrong.

"My father set his will up so *she*," his nose wrinkled in distaste, "and I have no choice but to live together for a year?"

"Yes," the lawyer confirmed. "He said if anything happened to him and Di, he wanted to be sure you both had family near."

"She's not my family," Lucas growled.

"But she is," Mr. Wilkinson insisted. "She's your step-sister."

"Get out," Lucas rasped.

I levered up and out of my chair, wanting nothing more than to get away and think.

"Not you," he hissed, wrapping a hand around my upper arm and holding me in place.

"Are you kicking me out of my own office?" Mr. Wilkinson asked.

"My step-sister," he barely gritted the word out, "and I need a moment alone to discuss our living arrangements."

I waited for the door to shut behind the lawyer before turning to glare up at Lucas. "There's an easy enough solution to all of this."

"Oh, yeah?" he drawled. "What's your bright idea, sweetheart?"

I felt a stab of pain in my heart at his scornful use of that particular term of endearment. The last time he'd called me sweetheart, he'd groaned it in my ear while telling me how good it felt to be inside me. I wasn't sure what I'd done to earn his disdain, but it only reinforced my decision. "I'm going to walk away from the inheritance."

"Sure you are," he scoffed. "Because after luring me into your bed in order to get me to give you an art show, you're the kind of woman who will walk away from several hundred million dollars."

*Several hundred million dollars? Whoa!*

"I can practically see the dollar signs in your eyes."

"First of all, *I* didn't lure *you* into my bed," I retorted, jabbing my finger into his sculpted chest. "You're the one who propositioned me."

"Like you weren't in my gallery with the express purpose of sleeping your way into a show," he muttered.

"The only reason I slept with you is because I wanted you," I seethed. "Forgive me for being stupid enough to be attracted to you. Don't worry, though. It won't happen again. I've learned my lesson where you're concerned."

It felt as though time stood still as we stared at each other. It wasn't my intention, but I'd thrown down a verbal gauntlet, one Lucas was quick to pick up. My heart raced in my chest when his eyes flared and he jerked me against his chest. I gasped in surprise, and he took advantage of the parting of my lips to drive his tongue into my mouth as he claimed it in a punishing kiss. He shifted forward, and I bumped into the desk behind me. Lifting me up, he roughly parted my thighs and settled my knees at his hips as my ass landed on top of the edge of the desk. My skirt rode up, bunching at my hips and exposing my panties.

His fingers headed straight for my core, shoving my panties out of the way before sinking deep. I was embarrassingly wet, but Lucas grunted in satisfaction as I moaned in pleasure. The hand at my hip disappeared, and I heard the sound of his zipper going down. It was quickly followed by the crinkle of foil, and then he drove inside me in one smooth thrust.

I buried my head in his shirt to muffle my screams as he thrust in and out, so hard I heard the desk creaking underneath me. This was an anger fuck, pure and simple. My head knew it, but my body didn't seem to care as I felt an orgasm quickly building. When one of his hands slid between us to pinch my clit, I flew apart, biting his chest in an effort to keep quiet.

"Fuck yes," he groaned. I felt the heat of his come as it filled the condom.

I was still shuddering, my pussy fluttering against him, when he pulled out of me and ripped the condom from his still-hard dick. He tied it off and glanced down at the trashcan full of my puke before shaking his head and shoving it into his pocket. After he had zipped his pants back up, he helped me down from the desk and watched me get my clothes straightened.

"*Now* you've learned your lesson. Don't make me teach it to you again, my darling step-sister," he murmured in my ear before releasing me to stride out of the office, slamming the door behind him.

I was befuddled from my orgasm, but I knew enough to understand Lucas was the last man I should be attracted to after the way he'd walked out on me, not to mention his reaction to seeing me today. And yet, none of that seemed to matter to my traitorous body. How in the world was I going to survive living with him for an entire year? And what the heck was I going to do if I was pregnant with his baby?

# Chapter 4

## LUCAS

It was utter, fucking bullshit! What was my dad thinking? He'd never even met the scheming, conniving, gold-digging, sexy, gorgeous... *Stop it right now!*

Not that I could actually cast the first stone at the moment, considering I'd just fucked my "step-sister" in the lawyer's office after he read my dad's will. Reaching the parking lot, I strode over to my car and stopped, placing my forehead on the cool surface. I was still overheated from our little sexcapade and burning with anger at myself, and my dad. I hadn't planned to touch her ever again, but the second she told me I'd never get another chance to fuck her, I couldn't help myself. I was driven by the need to prove her wrong, and prove to her and myself, that she was still as attracted to me as I was to her.

I guess I should be thankful for small mercies. At least he didn't give her half of the company. Whatever, if Dad wanted to play this game, I'd go along with it, if only so I could prove my theory about Jade and her mom correct. A possible solution popped into my head. If I pursued her, relentlessly, maybe kept her tied to my bed, *wait no, let's not cross into kidnapping territory.* But, if I made her uncomfortable enough, I might be able to get her to run. And, get some mind-blowing sex out of the deal.

The idea was shot down when I remembered the fucking board. Shit. There would be no hiding who she was from the media. They never stopped digging into my life. Being forced to live with her meant keeping our relationship platonic. We would have to play the part of step-siblings. Because, if the board got wind we were sleeping together, blood-related or not, it could cause a major scandal.

*Fuck! Fuck! Fuck!* Wrenching my car door open, I slid onto the black leather seat of my Ferrari. Turned it on and burnt rubber out of the lot. I returned to my penthouse in the city, leaving my car with the valet, and taking my private elevator to the top. After throwing my keys in the vicinity of the entry table, I went straight to the bar and poured myself a drink.

Looking around, I took in the sleek, modern design of my home. I never really cared for the way my place was decorated, but I was too busy to put any effort into changing it.

I'm not sure if I'd admit it to anyone else, but I preferred my ancestral home. It was warm and lived in, a mixture of comfortable and somewhat antique. My grandfather built the mansion and gave it to my parents as a wedding present. My childhood was spent there, my mother died there. She hadn't been able to get pregnant again until I was almost fourteen, but she and the baby were lost due to complications. I'd always known I would inherit it as their only living child.

Until my father decided to make sure I had "family" if anything ever happened to him. Well, I wasn't going to go down quietly. Jade could take her millions and get the fuck out of my life, but I would be keeping the house. Someday, when I decided to have kids, they would grow up there.

Finishing my drink, I put the glass in the sink, and called up a moving company. Then I packed a couple of bags and set off for my father's...no, it was *my* estate now that he was gone. Well, mine and Jade's for the time being, I thought darkly.

Once I arrived, I took my bags to the master suite and set them on the floor in the hallway. I stared at the closed door, memories of my childhood assaulting me. I hadn't been ready to go through my father's things yet, but I'd had everything stored neatly in the basement until the time was right.

Taking a deep breath, I opened the door and stepped inside. It looked the same, but without the small personal touches. He'd always joked about this room belonging only to the man of the house and his wife, not so subtly hinting that he was itching to pass it down to me. His way of telling me to get married and give him grandbabies.

I was ready to step into the role of the man of the house, even if I intended to occupy this room without a nagging wife. My saving grace was knowing my father hadn't moved the arm candy he'd just married in yet. To the best of my knowledge, she had never slept in this room.

I retrieved my suitcases from the hall and began to put things away. My solitude was eventually interrupted by the sound of someone at the open bedroom door.

"Oh, excuse me." Jade's sweet voice washed over me and my dick immediately hardened. Rather than turning from the closet with my obvious erection on display, I barked, "What do you want?"

The silence stretched a little too long and I wondered if she'd taken off, but when I turned around, she was still there, glaring at me.

"I was looking for a room to settle into, jackass. But, this house is a maze and I ended up here. So, you need to get down off that high and mighty horse, for which I'm sure he would be extremely grateful. It can't be easy carrying you *and* your ego around. And point me in the direction of the empty bedrooms, I'll get out of your space."

I pressed my lips together, making every effort not to either laugh or groan. She was fucking gorgeous when she was angry, those green eye full of fire, her spectacular tits bouncing with her rapid breaths, and her blonde hair hanging loose and wild around her. I stepped to the right where a small sitting area was set up and shielded my reaction to her behind a chair.

It was on the tip of my tongue to tell her to take the farthest bedroom in the opposite wing but when my mouth opened, that wasn't what came out.

"Your room is next door."

Jade gasped, "Surely there's another—"

"It's not up for discussion, Jade. The door to the right is your room," I said with authority. *What the fuck was wrong with me?* When I'd thought about her so far away, my mind and body both went on strike and started picketing the decision. My mouth was obviously the union leader because it had ordered her to sleep one wall away from me. Worse still, the rooms had a connecting door.

Mentally kicking my own ass, I knew I needed to get out of her presence. "If you'll excuse me, I have work to do." I stared at her meaningfully until she spun on her heel and marched into the next room. Once again able to breathe deeply, I waited for my hard-on to go down, as far as it ever would around Jade. Then I took off for the office located on the first floor.

Since I had no idea I would be moving in this quickly, the house was very understaffed. When my stomach started growling, I looked at the clock and was shocked to see it was already after seven.

I stood and stretched before wandering toward the kitchen to see if there was anything to make a decent meal out of, then laughed at myself. I couldn't cook worth shit, so I needed to find the menu drawer. Or start one.

As I neared the room, I heard music playing and someone moving around. At the door I stopped short, as though I'd run into a brick wall. Jade was dancing around the kitchen, her hips swinging, her body moving fluidly to the beat. I watched her in silence, the erotic picture in front of me making me lose all ability to think.

Then, as though from muscle memory, I was suddenly stalking her until I caught her, gripping her biceps and hauling her into my arms. Sucking her gasp of surprise into my mouth and replacing it with my tongue. All of my blood rushed to my groin and I groaned as I grew painfully hard.

My hands made their way down, over her tight ass, to the back of her thighs. I bent my knees and lifted her, guiding her legs around my waist and backing her up against the wall.

She moaned as I ground my cock into her pussy, shivers wracking her body. I needed her more than anything else at that moment. I reached for my zipper when a loud buzzer tore through my haze of lust. *What the fuck?*

Pulling back, I looked for the cause of the offending sound and recognized the cook timer on the stove was going off. Something was bubbling in a pot on top, and clearly a dish baking in the oven.

My stomach chose that minute to growl fiercely, reminding me it was empty. With the spell broken, I lowered Jade to the ground, doing my best to ignore her whimper of protest. I stepped back, my hands on her waist to steady her until she slapped at them, and I let go. She hurried over to the timer and shut it off, pulling from the oven what looked like ... freshly baked bread? No way.

This seemed like a scene from a movie, the little wife in the kitchen making her man dinner. Except this was anything but a movie, Jade was the last woman who would ever be my wife, and I wasn't sure she would be willing to share.

My stomach roared in protest and I considered the dangers of seducing some of this food out of her.

"I brought some groceries because I wasn't sure if the house was stocked," Jade said, stirring the pot and keeping her back to me. "Mr. Wilkinson explained nobody had been in residence. I was going to ask what you wanted to do about dinner, but I couldn't find you. "

She started hunting around and I finally snapped out of my trance, helping her to locate dishes and silverware.

"I made minestrone soup, salad is in the fridge, and there are fresh rolls. Help yourself." She was still avoiding my gaze and it was beginning to annoy me, but I worried about what I'd do if I looked into her intoxicating eyes. So, I helped myself to the food, put it on a tray, thanked her quietly, and ran to my office like a coward.

A little after midnight, I took my dishes to the kitchen, rinsed and put them in the dishwasher, then went up to my room. I hesitated at Jade's door, my hand itching to reach for the handle. Did she sleep in silky little nighties? Or a pair of boxers (I felt violent at the thought that she might be wearing another man's clothes) and a t-shirt? Or, I swallowed hard, in the nude?

I groaned and forced my feet to step one in front of the other until I was shut in my bedroom. Keeping my eyes anywhere but on the connecting door, I stripped and took an icy shower. After I had dried off, exhaustion hit me, and I practically stumbled to the bed and passed out.

Several hours later, I woke in the darkness from a distant sound. Instantly alert, I sat up and listened. It sounded like—well, like someone was getting sick. After a moment, I realized it was coming from Jade's ensuite bathroom. I threw the covers off and raced to her room.

# Chapter 5

## Jade

*Ugh! Could tonight get any worse?* Apparently it could, because another convulsion shook my body and I lost whatever contents remained in my stomach from dinner. Minestrone soup wasn't fun when it came back up, especially not when it had been paired with a salad.

Make that much, much worse. "Jade? Are you okay?" Lucas's question was spoken gently through the door, in a tone I hadn't heard from him since before he turned into an ass and stormed out of our hotel room.

"Do I sound like I'm fine?" I muttered under my breath.

The opening of the door was the only answer I got to a question he couldn't have possibly heard. Then he was on his knees behind me, one hand bunching my hair at the back of my neck while the other rubbed my back in soothing strokes. Jerky Lucas was hard enough to resist, I couldn't possibly expect myself to fare any better with this caring version of him. At least I didn't have to worry about falling victim to the chemistry between us anytime soon, since I felt like death warmed over and probably looked like it too.

When it seemed as though I was done, Lucas helped me to my feet and settled me on the stool in front of the vanity. The freaking vanity! This house was nothing like anywhere I'd ever lived before and I couldn't help but feel intimidated by the visible signs of wealth all around me. Well except maybe for the gourmet kitchen. It had truly been a joy to cook in there.

My stomach gurgled and I shoved all thoughts of food from my mind while taking the cold washcloth Lucas was handing me. Before I could use it, his hand was on my forehead, checking for a fever. I slapped it away and swiped the washcloth over my face.

"I don't think you have a fever." He sounded genuinely concerned. "And I ate the same dinner as you, so I don't think it's food poisoning."

I wished I was lucky enough to have food poisoning. "It's not."

"Maybe it was whatever you had for breakfast? That could explain why you were sick in Mr. Wilkinson's office earlier."

So could the baby I was beginning to think I was carrying. Not that I was going to tell him that, so I kept my mouth shut and let him continue.

"You should have made something lighter for dinner," he chided. "As much as I enjoyed the soup, chicken noodle would have been better if your stomach was still upset."

"Like you're the expert on what's good for me," I mumbled. "You don't even know me, not really. Or you wouldn't have said all those horrible things."

And, yep, those were tears welling in my eyes and streaming down my cheeks. *What the heck was wrong with me?* Oh, yeah. That's right. I was tired. I was also nauseous, but somehow hungry at the same time. Plus, I'd been stupid enough to pack a bag and move into the bedroom next to the man I'd let fuck me on a desk in a hoity-toity law office. An office belonging to the man who'd convinced me it wasn't just in my best interests to stay here but also Lucas's, and for some insane reason I actually cared. To top it all off, I was more hormonal than I'd ever been in my entire life. Probably because I'd missed my last period, not from the stress of my mother's death and my upcoming show, as I'd hoped, but due to the fact that I was almost definitely carrying Lucas's baby.

Who was now my step-brother.

Who I lived with.

In a mansion that I half-owned.

*Hysterics, here I came.*

Refusing to let him see how much of a mess I was, I kept the washcloth over my face while I tried to calm the heck down. Only Mr. Caring wasn't having any of that.

"Here, take this," he said gruffly, pulling the cloth out of my hand. I didn't look up at his face and instead focused on the toothbrush he was holding out for me. It was the one I'd put into the fancy holder on the marble countertop and he'd squirted some of my toothpaste onto it.

I shoved the brush into my mouth and scrubbed my teeth, avoiding inserting it too far for fear that it would start off another puking session. Once I was satisfied the taste was out of my mouth, I got to my feet and moved to the sink to spit and rinse. Lucas stayed nearby, leaning against the doorframe with his gaze on me the entire time. I finally realized what he was wearing, or um, not wearing, as the case was, since he was *naked*. I guessed I needed to add horny to the never-ending list of things I was feeling because the sight of his bare chest and other large, hard parts of him, put me straight back into a daze. And then I remembered what I was wearing, a pair of boyfriend shorts and a thin camisole. Cursing my fair coloring as I felt a blush sweep up my skin, I kept my eyes up while I brushed past Lucas and back into my bedroom.

Climbing back into bed, I pulled the covers over my body and kept my eyes on Lucas's face as he came closer. *Don't look down. Whatever you do, don't look down!*

"I'll call the family doctor and ask him to come see you first thing in the morning."

"I'm perfectly capable of making a doctor's appointment for myself." Because there was no way in the world I was going to let his doctor examine me. No way, no how.

"Then make one," he ordered, moving towards the door that connected our rooms. *Wait! There was a connecting door to our bedrooms? How had I not noticed this before?*

"I will!"

He stopped in the doorway. "And you'd better let me know what the doctor says."

"Of course I will. Right away, sir." *Liar.* If the doctor told me what I thought he was going to tell me, I was going to stall my butt off while I tried to find a way to give Lucas the news.

"You're pregnant."

The doctor's announcement shouldn't have come as a surprise considering why I was here, but I was still shocked. The receptionist had taken pity on me when I'd called to schedule and let me take the opening from a cancellation. It was a good thing, too, because I didn't think Lucas would have let me get away with not seeing his doctor for more than a day. And the last thing I wanted was to have to try to convince some doctor I'd never met to keep my pregnancy a secret until I was ready to talk to Lucas about it.

He already thought I was an opportunist who'd tried to trick him into giving her an art show. And a gold-digger. Apparently, he could add whatever it is people call women who get pregnant on purpose for money to the list. Not that I'd done this on purpose or wanted anything from him. But I was sure he'd see it that way because I'd been subject to his harsh judgment twice before. I wasn't thrilled at the prospect of going through it again. Especially not knowing whether this was going to happen for the rest of my life since we were going to have a child together.

I tried to focus on what the doctor told me about how far along I was and how their office handled pregnancy appointments. I retained maybe half of what she said, scheduled my next appointment and then made it to the safety of my car.

*I was pregnant.*

I let the thought really sink in. My mom and dad were both dead, and I'd never been close to my extended family since they were spread across the country. My hand cradled my stomach protectively, and I was in awe of the idea that I was going to be a mother.

A baby was growing inside me. One I was going to raise. Someone I'd love unconditionally. A life I'd do anything to protect, starting with whatever it took to fulfill the terms of my step-father's will to ensure this child had anything they'd ever need, even if Lucas decided he wanted nothing to do with us.

I made a couple stops along the way back to my new home. I tiptoed into the house and softly closed the door behind me, hoping beyond hope that Lucas wouldn't hear me come in. I had the bag from the pharmacy in one hand, filled with anti-nausea meds and prenatal vitamins. In the other, I had one from the bookstore with several pregnancy books inside. I might not have planned to get pregnant, but I intended to be the best pregnant woman ever now that I knew I was.

"What did the doctor say?" Lucas's question came out of nowhere.

I turned quickly and found him standing under the archway which separated the foyer from a formal sitting room with a window overlooking the front drive. He must have been waiting for me to get home. I felt the blood drain from my face and grabbed for the doorknob as spots danced in front of my eyes. *Crap! What the heck was I going to tell him? And how in the world was I going to stop myself from passing out?*

## Chapter 6

## LUCAS

I lunged forward and caught Jade right before she hit the ground. My heart was beating out of my chest. I'd worried about her all day, then she finally arrived home and passed out in my arms. I stopped pretending I wasn't worried.

Scooping her up, I hooked her bags on my fingers and started up the wide staircase, taking the stairs two at a time. At the top, it split into two hallways, one on either side, both open with a railing allowing a view down into the foyer below. I turned down the right hall and without thought, took her into my room and set her gently on the bed, dropping her bags on the dresser. What the fuck kind of a doctor had she seen? He was clearly a quack if he sent her home like this.

Her eyelids started to flutter and I quickly retrieved a damp washcloth from the bathroom to cool her forehead as she came to. I was still vacillating on whether or not I should call nine-one-one when her beautiful green eyes were suddenly staring at me, swimming with fear. She was obviously as worried about her fainting episode as I was.

"Sweetheart. What did the doctor tell you?" I asked softly, keeping my voice low in case her head was bothering her.

She looked around before asking, "Why am I in your room?"

I hadn't even realized I'd come straight to my bed. "Force of habit," I lied. I'd brought her in here because it felt natural, like this was where she was supposed to be.

"I'll take you back to your room." I started to lift her into my arms again but she pushed my hands away.

"I can walk—"

I grabbed her wrists and held them in front of her with one hand, the other going under her ass to lift her up. "I'll carry you," I said firmly, my tone brokering no argument.

She remained silent, which was probably a good thing because if I had to get her to stop talking again, there was a good chance I'd be using my mouth to do it and I wouldn't be telling her to be quiet.

Once I had her settled, I sat on the bed next to her and her eyebrows rose to her hairline with surprise. "So?" I demanded.

She closed her eyes and sighed. "Could we maybe talk about this when I'm not so woozy? I think I just need to rest for a while."

I wanted to argue, but the faint purple shadows under her eyes convinced me she needed rest and my inquisition could wait. I brushed some of her hair off of her forehead, resisting the temptation to place a kiss there. "Alright, we'll talk after you've slept for a bit."

I stood and padded to the door, leaving the room and shutting it quietly behind me. Then I strode purposefully into my bedroom and pulled my cell phone from my pocket, pacing as I put a call into my family doctor. I didn't care what she said, she was going to be checked out by a physician I knew and trusted.

Hanging up my phone, I dropped it on the dresser and noticed the bags Jade had brought in with her. I picked them up intending to sneak into her room and leave them where she would be able to find them. I must have grabbed the wrong end because the contents of one of the bags slipped out and crashed onto the floor, making a racket despite landing on plush cream carpet. I squatted down and picked up the bottles, only glancing at their labels for a second.

The room started spinning and I lost my balance, my ass hitting the ground hard, the bottle rattling in my hand.

*Prenatal Vitamins.*

It didn't take a genius to know what those were for. Was Jade pregnant? With another man's baby? A slow burn started in my belly and I felt fury building. But another part of me knew it was more likely the baby was mine. Was it? No, we'd worn condoms. Every—*oh fuck.* I'd gotten carried away and fucked her bare in the shower.

The room stopped spinning, in fact, the world stopped rotating, time halted, and I'm pretty sure even the angels in heaven stopped singing. I've never experienced such utter stillness and quiet. All the better to hear the screaming in my head. One part howling with anger and one part a caveman beating on his chest in triumph.

I was torn, still struggling with my belief that she was using me for my money and position as owner of the gallery. Yet, the signs indicating I'd been wrong were piling up. Why hadn't she asked about the gallery showing?

My mind played over her reactions at the lawyer's office, once again. Could her shock have been genuine? Then she'd bought groceries and made us dinner, without being asked, or demanding reimbursement. Of course, it's not like she needs the money anymore, right? She's gotten exactly what she wanted. I think. I sighed and scratched my head, the whole situation was like a rollercoaster and I couldn't figure out which way was up.

I emptied her other bag to find books about pregnancy, but looking at them was making me nauseous. I'm aware of the irony. Putting everything back in the bags, I clutched them tight, not ready to let them go, as though if I did, it would cease to be real. Moving my pacing to the front hall, I anxiously waited for the doctor to arrive.

An hour later, I'd worn a hole in the damn floor waiting for Dr. Morgan. I asked him to wait in the informal family room located through another arched doorway near the stairwell, while I checked on Jade. Realizing I was still holding the books and medicine, I dropped the items on a table in the entryway and jogged up the stairs to her room. I knocked softly and listened for any sound indicating she was awake.

I heard shuffling and the door opened revealing a deliciously mussed Jade. Damn, she looked adorable and so fuckable at the same time. She looked a little green and had a hand over her flat stomach. A vision of Jade with her hand resting on a swollen belly flashed before my eyes. She looked beautiful.

"Have you seen the, um, bags I brought home with me?" she asked, breaking me out of my daydream. Her voice was hesitant, but her green eyes were flared with worry. Was she ever intending to tell me? I was becoming rather confused. Why wouldn't she have announced it right away and demanded I marry her? I couldn't let her take all of the blame for her condition, but I was shocked she wasn't trying to use it as leverage to trap me.

It suddenly occurred to me, was it because I was technically her step-brother? Tension wrapped itself around my heart as I considered the possibility she might fight for me to not be a part of my child's life. No. That wasn't going to happen. As soon as I could get control away from the current board at work, I'd be marrying her ass if I had to drag her to the courthouse, kicking and screaming. Until then, we'd have to keep it a secret and stay under the radar.

"I left them on the table in the foyer." I held my hand out to her, "Come, my family doctor, Dr. Morgan, is waiting for you downstairs. I want him to have a look at you."

Her green eyes grew impossibly wide, "What?" she shrieked. "Bu—but, I already saw a doctor!"

I huffed in annoyance, "Your doctor obviously didn't know what the fuck they were doing. They sent you home and you fainted. Not to mention, you look as though you're about to lose your stomach again."

I took her hand instead of waiting for her to reach for mine and started towing her behind me, intent on getting her to Dr. Morgan.

She tugged weakly, trying to get me to release her, but I disregarded her efforts.

"My doctor is fine. She sent me home with medicine, I just need my pills, not to see another physician."

We reached the stairs and I immediately started to worry about her fainting again and taking a spill, possibly hurting herself or the baby. I swung her up into my arms, ignoring her when she protested.

"Jade," I said, my voice a little patronizing. "The sooner you stop arguing and let Dr. Morgan look you over, the sooner I'll stop harassing you about it."

Her eyes narrowed and she gave me a glacial stare, until it once again caved under the weight of my stubbornness.

"Fine, but no blood tests or anything invasive. Just a standard checkup," she finished as I crossed the threshold into the room where Dr. Morgan had set out his instruments.

"She needs a blood test," I informed Dr. Morgan as I set her down on the overstuffed couch. I threw her a black look when she started to comment and it shut her up.

"And who have we here?" Dr. Morgan smiled at Jade, "Does this beautiful woman belong to you, Lucas?"

"No," Jade answered before I could even open my mouth. She returned my angry expression with a somewhat sly smile. "I'm his step-sister, Jade."

I had no clue how to respond. Did I tell the doctor about our history and trust him to keep it a secret? Or did I pretend the baby wasn't mine and we were simply cohabitating step-siblings? I wanted to shout and punch something. This whole situation was so fucked up.

"Really? I didn't realize Jonathan's new wife had a daughter. It's lovely to meet you." He smiled and shook her hand. If he weren't here to examine her, I might have ripped off his appendage for touching her. No one else will ever be caressing her silky skin but me ever again.

"We didn't know about each other until recently," she admitted.

"Really? Well, how wonderful you two aren't left without family."

His comment made me cringe, much too similar to the words of my father's will, which put me in this ridiculous spot in the first place.

"Now, what seems to be the problem, my dear?" Dr. Morgan asked as he began taking her blood pressure.

"She's been nauseous, exhausted, and she fainted earlier," I growled, glowering at Jade as I started to pace again.

"Any chance you're pregnant, Jade?"

I waited with baited breath to see how she would answer.

She cleared her throat, "Um." She glanced at me and Dr. Morgan took notice.

"Lucas, perhaps you should wait in another room."

Jade smiled triumphantly.

"I need to be here. With our parents gone, I'm her legal guardian. Our parents wanted someone to take care of her." I grinned back at Jade.

"Puh-lease. I'm twenty-two years old. And even if I wasn't, nobody would pick you to guard their dog, much less another human being." Her cheeks brightened with color as we bantered back and forth.

"Now, now, Jade, you mustn't compare yourself to a puppy, at least you're house trained."

She huffed and Dr. Morgan chuckled. "Squabbling like siblings already."

Our matching gasps of disgust seemed to shock the doctor and his gaze bounced between us like a pinball machine. After a tense moment, he focused back on Jade as he got her arm ready for a blood draw.

"Ugh. Another needle, I think I'm going to be sick again."

"You know," I drawled, "You didn't answer the doctor's question."

Jade's eyes flew to me and I smiled sinisterly. "Any chance you could be pregnant Jade?"

"Yes," she snapped. "I had a fling with a macho, egotistical, shallow, pompous ass who apparently didn't know how to use a fucking condom and knocked me up. That's why the blood test isn't necessary because my doctor already confirmed it this morning."

I didn't know why but hearing her admit it out loud made the whole thing much more real. Holy fuck. I'd gotten Jade pregnant. Mentally banging my head against a wall, I amended the thought. I'd gotten my step-sister pregnant. The board was going to ruin me and send me off to live in Louisiana with all of the other people whose lives sing like a fucking country song.

# Chapter 7

## Jade

*Had I really said what I thought I did?* Someone please tell me I hadn't. I slowly opened my eyes, which I'd squeezed shut in mortification as soon as the words popped out of my mouth. *Yup, I'd totally said exactly what I thought I had.* The twin looks of shock on Lucas and the doctor's faces confirmed it.

"I guess we won't need a blood test after all," the doctor drawled, placing the needle down right before jabbing me with it. It was the only upside to my untimely announcement. He got over his surprise more quickly than Lucas, who stood there staring at me with his jaw open and his eyes wide. Dr. Morgan's attention shifted between the two of us before focusing on Lucas. "While I appreciate your concern for your step-sister, I think it would be better if you gave us some privacy to discuss such a delicate matter."

Privacy sounded fantastic to me, but I couldn't bear the tormented look on

Lucas's face at the doctor's request. I'd pulled the rug out from under him with my announcement, and it wouldn't be fair of me to make him wait in another room so soon afterward.

"It's okay," I sighed. "He can stay."

"If you're sure?" Dr. Morgan's tone was doubtful, but I appreciated him giving me another out if I wanted to take it. Lucas didn't welcome it, though.

"You heard Jade," he growled, prowling over to me, taking my hand in his and squeezing tightly.

Lucas turned towards me as soon as we heard the sound of the front door closing. "The baby's mine?"

I wanted to scream and cry at the very thought of him suspecting it was someone else's, but I couldn't blame him for the question. It wasn't even an accusation, he was merely asking for confirmation of what I had hinted to when the doctor was present. "Yes."

His gaze dropped to my stomach and I swore I saw triumph in his eyes, which made no sense at all considering his opinion of me. "Okay, this isn't necessarily a bad thing. In a way, you being pregnant simplifies things," he mumbled to himself, pacing the length of the room.

"How is my pregnancy simple?"

Instead of answering, he shocked me speechless by striding over to me and lifting me up in his arms. He swiftly made his way through the house, up the stairs and into his bedroom, placing me gently on the mattress. Then he quickly stripped out of his clothes, only leaving his boxers, and climbed in next to me.

I was about to object, my lips ready to form the words, when he stopped to place a soft kiss on my belly. The gesture was so darn sweet, I all but melted into the mattress. By the time he settled himself on the pillows with me in his arms, I was a strange combination of an emotional mess and a beyond horny as heck woman.

"Your pregnancy means I don't need to fight this thing between us anymore."

I couldn't help but laugh, considering we'd spent a grand total of five days together over the last six weeks and had slept together all but one of those days—today. Based on the fact that I was lying on his bed next to him in only his boxers, it was pretty safe to assume we were about to keep the streak alive. "I think your definition of fighting our chemistry and mine are very different. And I don't understand why you've felt the *need* in the first place."

His arms tightened around me. "The circumstances surrounding our first meeting were suspicious."

"An artist meeting a gallery owner in their place of business is *not* suspicious."

"It is if she looks like you and agrees to spend the weekend in a hotel with me without so much as a single word in protest."

"You're the one who suggested it," I grumbled. "What did you want me to do? Say no?"

His eyes lit with humor. "I'm not sure it would have mattered if you'd said no. I would have just found a way to get you to say yes at some point."

"So you don't still think I tried to sleep my way into a show at your gallery?" I asked, placing a finger over his lips while I hurried to finish what I wanted to say. "A show I didn't need any help in getting all by myself at another well-respected gallery, mind you. My art stands on its own, and even if it didn't, I'm not about to prostitute myself to *anyone* for *anything*."

He jolted, his eyes lighting with a possessive gleam, as though I'd just issued a challenge. "Damn straight you're not. Nobody gets to touch you but me."

"Am I to presume this means you won't go around assuming I'm giving some poor, unsuspecting guy a blow job if I need to puke and his trash can is the conveniently nearby?"

He ducked his head and I swore I saw a sweep of red tinting his cheeks. "I'm sorry," he mumbled.

"Could you repeat that? I'm pretty sure I didn't hear you right," I teased.

"I'm sorry," he repeated more firmly this time, his head jerking up so he stared directly into my eyes. "I should have let you explain before storming out of the hotel room six weeks ago, and I shouldn't have accused you of what I did in the lawyer's office."

*Holy heck*, he'd apologized. But that didn't mean I couldn't jerk his chain a little more. "How do I know you don't think I'm just a call-girl for your exclusive use?"

"Because the only payment you've taken is all the orgasms I've given you." His hand drifted down to my belly. "And my baby." Then he went about showing me exactly how he'd give me those orgasms, stripping my clothes from my body and taking the time to cup each of my breasts, rolling the nipples between his fingertips. He trailed kisses down my chest until he reached my breasts. His tongue flicked against one of my nipples before he sucked it into his mouth. Releasing it with a loud pop, he switched his attention to the other side.

"Lucas," I whimpered. My breasts had always been sensitive, but they were even more so now. I felt the pull of his mouth on my nipple all the way down in my pussy.

"What, sweetheart?" he purred.

"I need to come."

"I'm going to make you come, Jade. Have patience and know I'll get you there," he promised before moving lower and nipping lightly at the skin on my belly. My hips jerked in response, my pussy bumped against his hard length. I felt the heat of his skin through the fabric of his boxers and moaned in need.

Lucas gripped my thighs, holding them open as he bent over my pussy. His breath was hot against my core, his tongue flicking against my clit and dipping lower to slide inside.

"Tastes so damn good," he murmured against my damp flesh before he started to fuck me with his tongue. One of his hands slid up my thigh and across my belly, moving down again to play with my clit. After a few flicks of his finger, he pinched it and I went off like a rocket. I shuddered beneath him while he licked me through my orgasm.

"Holy crap," I whispered when I managed to stop panting and was able to speak.

I watched, entranced by the sight of his muscles bunching when Lucas levered up to shove his boxers down. His cock sprang free, long and hard, before he settled himself between my legs.

"I need you, sweetheart, but I'll try to be as gentle as I can."

I reached up to rest my palm on his cheek. "Take me however you want, Lucas. You're not going to hurt the baby."

My permission seemed to snap the last of his control. He slammed his cock into me with a hard thrust. I was swollen from my climax and my pussy clenched around him as he pulled back out to dive in again.

"Always so damn good," he groaned.

"The best," I agreed.

His eyes heated at my words and he pounded into me harder and faster. "Come for me again, Jade. I don't think I can hold on much longer. Your pussy feels too perfect wrapped around my cock."

I circled my legs around his waist as he continued to hammer into me. It only took a couple more thrusts before I went over the edge again, taking him with me.

"Damn, Jade," he muttered. "That was fucking amazing. I don't know how the hell we're going to hide what's between us when all I want to do is take you like this every time I'm near you."

"Hide?" I repeated, hoping I misunderstood what he'd said because my heart was still pounding loudly.

"We can't tell anyone," he replied, his tone matter-of-fact, as though what he was saying was obvious to anyone with a brain.

*Say what now?* "What do you mean, we can't tell anyone? Who the heck do you think I'm going to tell? The newspapers? Because I'm not! The only person I want to talk to right now is my best friend, and she sure as heck isn't going to go blabbing to anyone about my pregnancy."

"I'm not accusing you of anything, sweetheart."

"Not yet, anyway," I muttered, thinking about how quickly he'd turned on me back at the hotel when he assumed I'd been using him to move up in the art world.

"It's complicated, Jade," he sighed. "There's the company to consider. I need time to finagle some things before anyone can know about us. The board is quite conservative. I'm confident they wouldn't appreciate the possible scandal associated with their new CEO getting his step-sister pregnant."

I nodded my head like I understood and offered him a little tilt of my lips which I hoped resembled a smile. Then I yawned widely and rolled away from him, waiting until he couldn't see my face to allow my tears to stream down my cheeks and onto the pillow. Pregnant and unmarried I could handle. The baby and I being his dirty little secret? Not so much.

## Chapter 8

## LUCAS

I'd fucked Jade hard after she'd already been sick and exhausted all day, so when she turned over, I let her get some sleep. I smoothed a hand down over her silky blonde hair and traced circles on her naked back as I ran scenarios in my head. I needed to move up the timetable and get a new board in place as quickly as possible. I intended to marry Jade in the next couple of weeks, but we'd have to keep it quiet. Something I wasn't at all happy about, but it was necessary for the moment. However, when my baby was born, both he or she and their mother were going to have my name. And, hiding it from the paparazzi would be near impossible with both Jade's and my name on the birth certificate.

I sighed in frustration, my feet itching to pace. Checking Jade's breathing, the soft, even rhythm told me she was sleeping peacefully, so I slipped out of bed. As quietly as possible, I dressed and went down to my office. I didn't do well with chaos, I never had. Plans, lists, organization, these were what kept my life on track.

Sitting down at the large, cherry wood desk, I took a minute to remember all the days I'd wandered in here as a kid. My dad would be hard at work on his computer, or leaning back in his chair reading, with a cigar in his hand. Whatever he was doing, he would stop and smile, beckoning me toward him. He'd ask about my day, or give me a little something to do. I always felt welcome. There were many times when I would simply sit on the couch across from him and watch him work. I was so in awe of him, so proud of him.

Maybe, *maybe*, he knew more about Di than I'd realized. Or, maybe she was exactly what I assumed and I was only wrong about Jade. I was more comfortable with option B, I didn't like being wrong.

Firing up the computer, I spent a couple of hours researching and making a list for my assistant. I wanted the house to be the best environment for Jade and our baby. I instructed him to hire a chef familiar with what pregnant women should and shouldn't eat, a delivery of vitamins and supplements Jade should (according to my research) be taking, a company to come in and baby-proof the house, a live-in pre-natal nurse, and an upgraded security system. The list continued to grow, so I told him to delegate some of it out. I also called *my* attorney and had him draw up a non-disclosure for the new employees. I always required one to be signed, but it was even more necessary considering the precarious state of our relationship.

Feeling accomplished, and much more in control, I shut off my computer and stretched. My stomach rumbled and I checked my watch, it was almost six. I'd let Jade sleep for a little more than three hours, but I was sure she'd be hungry soon. She and the baby needed to eat.

I was reaching for my phone when it started ringing.

"St. James," I answered gruffly, annoyed at being interrupted when all I wanted to do was feed Jade and take her back to bed.

"Lucas, my boy!" I stifled an irritated sigh at the sound of Charles Finlay, one of, if not the most stuffy and self-righteous ass on the board of my company.

"What can I do for you, Finlay?" I asked, valiantly attempting to sound professional instead of sulky.

"We're having a get-together at the L'étang tomorrow night. I know it's late notice, but I'm hoping you'll join us. We want to introduce you to some of our clients."

Fuck. This was a golden opportunity to get to know the heads of the companies I would be trying to convince to stay with mine when I booted out the 'Good Ole' Boys Club.' I really needed to attend, but I didn't want to leave Jade.

"I'm not sure if I can—"

"Make sure you bring a date. We'll see you at nine," he interrupted, as though I hadn't begun to decline, then promptly hung up.

My hand gripped the phone hard, my knuckles turning white. I needed to go since his request for me to bring a date was actually a semi-politely worded demand. These men liked their own kind and showing up younger, richer, single, and without a date would do nothing to bridge the already wide gap between us professionally. Some of them would be bringing their wives, but many of them would be with a girlfriend or, more likely, their current mistress. *Conservative family men, my ass.* It's all about appearances with them, and a mistress is much less fodder for the tabloids than being in a relationship with your step-sibling. Although, to be fair, not all of them were such hypocrites.

I certainly couldn't take Jade and I wasn't about to take another woman. *Damn it!* I was about to toss my cell at the wall when I heard a soft knock. I looked up to see Jade lounging in the open doorway. She looked tousled and sleepy in one of my t-shirts, fucking adorable. Seeing her there, wearing my clothes, made the possessiveness I felt for her jump up about ten notches.

"Hey," she greeted softly, "Everything alright?"

I smiled tightly, as tension built in my muscles. "Sure. Are you hungry?"

Her eyes lit up and she smiled brightly. "Starved."

I laughed and crooked a finger at her before patting my lap. She rolled her eyes, but padded over and curled up in my arms.

My hand began rubbing circles on her back and I kissed the top of her head. "What would you like to eat?"

"Mmmmm...I could really go for a nice, juicy, steak."

The little moan had my cock digging into her round little ass. One more moan like that and I could not be held responsible for my actions.

Steak? Her food choice broke into my thoughts. Maybe... No, what a stupid idea.

"Have you ever been to L'étang?" I asked, then immediately wanted to kick myself. *Shut the fuck up, St. James.*

"The steakhouse?" Her voice was incredulous as she leaned back to stare at me. "It's like one thousand dollars a plate!"

I chuckled and shook my head. "Exaggerate much?"

She smiled and shrugged.

*Ask her what she wants to order in.* "I have a last minute work thing there tomorrow night. Want to go with me?" *What the actual fuck, man?* I almost winced at the voice screaming at me in my head. Yeah, that was stupid.

She hadn't returned to her spot tucked into my chest. Her head was still up and she was studying me.

"As your date?" she asked cautiously.

*Tread carefully.* "Well, no. I can't have *you* as my date."

Her green eyes began to cloud with a dark emotion. *Way to go, now get your foot out of your mouth.*

I went on quickly, "Obviously, I'm not going to take *any* date. If I did, it would, of course, be you. I can't go alone, though, not with this crowd anyway."

Her face warned me of an impending storm, a riot of feelings I couldn't quite nail down.

She raised an eyebrow. "So, you want to take me, but you can't?"

Ah. No wonder, I wasn't being very clear. I smiled, certain she'd be happy when I explained I'd still be taking her with me. "I wouldn't have invited you if I didn't intend to take you, sweetheart. You'll accompany me as my step-sister. A sibling is always an acceptable substitute for a date."

The dark emotions in her eyes turned into a full-blown black cloud and she jumped off my lap. Rounding on me, she slammed her fists onto her hips. Let's be clear, I was doing my very best to pay attention, but when her large tits were bouncing at eye level because she was breathing heavy, it was impossible for me to keep from drifting to thoughts of sex. I was a man. She's got fucking amazing tits. Not my fault. Case closed.

Apparently, Jade was not aware of this ruling because she snapped her fingers in front of my eyes and yelled, "My eyes are up here, jackass."

I dragged my gaze up to her fiery green one, blazing with hurt and anger. I reared back a little at the intensity.

"You want to take me, the woman who is *pregnant with your baby*, to a work function and introduce me as your *step-sister*?" she shrilled.

Shifting uncomfortably, I grumbled, "Well, when you say it like that."

"How would you say it, Lucas?"

I sighed, "I want to be with you, Jade. Out in the open. This dinner gets us one step closer to making that possible. It would be better if I took a date, but I can get away with bringing my new-found family member."

She was still fuming, so I smiled and gently grasped her wrist, bringing her back to my lap. She reluctantly obliged and I wrapped my arms around her.

"I'm sorry, sweetheart. Will you please come with me?"

# Chapter 9

## Jade

I shouldn't have let Lucas off the hook so easily. I was a strong woman, one who'd proven she was able to stand on her own two feet. Yet, I crumbled anytime it came to him. Self-control was a thing of the past whenever I was near him. It had been from the first moment we'd met. Clothes flew off my body at the drop of a hat and yes seemed to be the only word I was capable of saying. He'd practically called me a gold-digger and I let him take me on a desk without a single word of apology. Then he told me I couldn't go to his elegant business dinner as his date, even though we'd spent an amazing afternoon together after learning I was pregnant with his baby. My response should have been heck no, but instead I'd said yes, gone out the next day, bought a fancy dress, and got my hair, makeup and nails done.

I'd wanted to look my best, even if I was only attending the dinner as Lucas's step-sister and not his date. Judging by the look on his face as I walked down the stairs, it was well worth all the effort. Before my foot hit the bottom step, he was moving towards me.

"Are you sure you want to have dinner out with my boring board members instead of a night home alone with me?" His question was said in a teasing tone, but the intense look in his eyes was anything but a joke. The way his fingers gripped my hips as he pulled me closer made me think he might toss me over his shoulder and carry me up to his bedroom. When I was flush against him, the feel of his hardened length told me exactly how we'd end up spending the night if I said I wanted to stay home.

I could always wear the dress another night. "Let's—"

My answer was drowned out by the sound of my growling stomach. The anti-nausea medication was working its magic, and I was starving.

"That sounds like a resounding yes for dinner," Lucas said with a chuckle.

I grumbled a little as he led me to the car. I hadn't really gotten a vote, but apparently the sex marathon idea was out and a steak dinner was in. Or maybe I'd get lucky and I could have both. The night was still young after all.

A mere two hours later, I wasn't as hopeful. *Was this night ever going to end?* When we arrived at L'étang, Lucas escorted me around the private room and introduced me to everyone as his stepsister. This meant I couldn't visibly react when several of the women present practically devoured him with their eyes even as they held onto the arms of their own dates. I didn't object when he got me settled in my seat and then left me there to go talk business with a small group of men huddled in the corner before dinner was served.

The meal was spent with the men discussing business while the women pushed their food around their plates and looked pretty. Except for me. I enjoyed the heck out of my ridiculously expensive steak. After dessert had been served, the men excused themselves for an after-dinner drink at the bar. Lucas gave my hand the briefest of squeezes before joining them. I tried to take comfort in the small gesture and to remind myself that the situation was only temporary, but what I'd really wanted to do was hold tight and make him stay with me. I couldn't do that and it killed me. What sister would mind if her brother left her side after all?

*Oh, just the kind whose step-brother knocked her up, that's who.* I snort giggled into my hand at my own joke, glancing around and hoping I didn't catch anyone's attention. It was too much to wish for, though, because a guy was staring at me from across the room. I quickly looked away, my gaze dropping to what was left of my dessert. Not just mine, Lucas's too since he'd been incredibly sweet and told me to order the chocolate soufflé and he'd gotten the crème brûlée so I didn't have to choose. He'd barely taken a bite of his dessert before nudging it my way. Although any goodwill he'd earned from the gesture had been used up within the last thirty minutes or so.

Another glance up confirmed that his business colleague was nearing me. Maybe I'd drawn this guy's attention because I was the only woman eating anything at this shindig. A glance out of the side of my eye told me that wasn't the right guess. He was striding towards me, the speculative gleam in his eye making me uncomfortable. Did he know about Lucas and me? Was he going to cause trouble for the company? Crap, when was

Lucas coming back anyway? I glanced frantically around the room hoping he'd returned from smoking a cigar on the terrace.

"It's a shame to see a gorgeous woman like you sitting alone."

Double crap. Still no sign of Lucas. On the plus side, it didn't look like this guy had come over here for nefarious purposes. He'd come to flirt with Lucas's step-sister, who was single and most definitely *not* pregnant with her step-brother's baby. I took a deep breath to calm my nerves and smoothed the skirt of my dress so it covered my thigh since his eyes were locked on the bare skin showing there. On second thought, fixing my dress might not have been my best decision tonight because his gaze moved from my legs to my boobs. They'd always caught guys' attention since they'd practically appeared overnight in high school. With them being slightly bigger from the pregnancy already, they were even more of a guy magnet. I was also regretting my choice in dress as he claimed Lucas's chair and stared at my chest.

"You're Jade, right?"

I cleared my throat, drawing his gaze up to my face. The grin he gave me was unapologetic, and kind of bordering on sleazy. "Yup, that's me."

"I'm Charles Montgomery the third."

He sounded like a pompous ass! One who'd taken hold of my hand and was tracing circles in the palm with one of his fingers.

"I'd like my hand back, please."

His hold tightened when I tried to tug it away. Better make that an aggressive, arrogant ass.

"And I'd like to keep it," he murmured. "How about we come to a deal of some kind. I'm sure I can persuade you to my way of thinking."

"I'm not interested," I hissed, tugging harder. His hold became painful, making me cringe. "Please," I whimpered.

"Now that's a word I'd like to hear you say, but in a more private setting." My stomach churned as he leaned in closer. The smell of scotch on his breath was overwhelming. "We both know I've got exactly what a girl like you wants in a man. A fat wallet and an even fatter—"

He didn't get the chance to finish his offensive comment. Lucas had returned and jerked him out of his chair by the collar of his shirt. "What the fuck do you think you're doing, Montgomery?"

"Nothing that concerns you, St. James. The girl and I were just coming to an understanding."

Lucas's gaze swept me up and down, checking to make sure I was okay. Fury flared in his eyes when he caught sight of me holding my wrist gingerly. I jumped up from my chair when he pulled Charles even closer.

"It looks like Jade wants nothing to do with you or your understanding. So how about you keep your hands off her."

"Please," Charles sputtered. "A woman like her wouldn't be offended by my offer. I was going to be very generous with her."

"Shut the fuck up before I make you," Lucas growled.

"Why are you so pissed off?" As crazy as it seemed, Charles looked like he truly didn't understand Lucas's anger. "You should be happy to get her off your hands after the way her mother trapped your father into marriage."

I gasped in outrage at the slight to my mom, the sound reminding both men of my presence.

"You know what? I don't have time for this shit." Lucas punctuated his statement with a sharp jab to Charles's chin, releasing his collar and letting him fall to the ground. Then he reached for me and ushered me out of the room.

Lucas had fully explained his situations and concerns before I completely agreed to attend the dinner. I was pretty sure his plan to lure clients on his own without the help of his current board had been thrown out the window. Practically dragging me from the most expensive restaurant in town while threatening a colleague and punching him in the face probably wasn't the best way to earn anyone's business

## Chapter 10

## LUCAS

I kept a firm grip on Jade's hand, dragging her away from the lecherous asshole who'd had the nerve to touch what was mine. Glancing behind to make sure I wasn't going too fast, my eyes once again skimmed over her.

When she had walked down the steps earlier in the evening (informing me it was the only way to make a grand entrance), she'd taken my breath away. Her platinum hair was pulled back into a long, straight ponytail, showing off her neck, with sparkling studs in her ears. Her collarbone and shoulders were bare save for the tiny straps of her emerald green dress. The rest of the shimmery fabric molded to her body, those unbelievable curves, making my mouth water. The dress fell to just above her knees, but there was a peeking split on her left side going up higher than I was comfortable with.

I'd managed to keep my trap shut and deal with it, not wanting to spoil what would probably be the only good thing about her evening besides an outrageously expensive steak. It had taken all of my strength to walk out the door instead of sweeping her back upstairs to the bedroom.

After watching these assholes drool over her and being forced to pretend I didn't care, I was already at a breaking point. But, to walk up to her being propositioned was more than I could take.

Before we reached the front of the restaurant, I'd texted my driver to come and pick us up. Nights like these, I always had a driver so I could drink with my colleagues. However, I'd been doing my best to dazzle Jade and I'd brought her in a stretch limousine. She'd laughed and told me I was being too over the top, but the excited twinkle in her green eyes confirmed I'd made the right choice.

Within minutes of arriving outside, the limo came to a stop at the curb, and we slipped inside. I tugged Jade close to me on the bench seat and picked up the phone to speak with the driver.

"Back to the house." Jade shifted and her tits pressed against my side, causing my pants to be in serious jeopardy of shredding around the teeth of the zipper.

"Take the long way," I snapped and tossed the phone back into its cradle.

Without wasting any more time, I grasped her small waist and lifted her over my lap, so she was straddling me. Our mouths connected and the temperature in the enclosed space exploded. She tasted like chocolate and caramel, her body was warm and pliant in my arms. Before I lost all sense of logic, my arm flopped around beside me until it found the button for the privacy screen and I heard it whoosh into place.

Working my mouth down her neck, one of my hands lowered the zipper on the back of her dress, while the other dropped a strap off of her shoulder. I kissed the bare spot while the loosening of her dress allowed me to pull the top down to her waist, freeing her heavy, naked tits. Then my hands cupped the globes, lifting them up as an offering and I latched onto one of her hard, pink nipples.

She cried out and rocked against me. I remembered everything about our first weekend together, especially how sensitive her nipples had been. But, the last few times we'd fucked, it was like they were ten times more so and I vaguely wondered if I could make her come just from playing with them.

It was a test for another day, though. I was so far gone, I was almost feral, sucking and biting a nipple with my mouth, while my fingers toyed with the other. Jade's sweet cries and her strong grip on my head urged me to continue to torture her.

I backed away suddenly and set her back so she was resting on the edge of my knees. She looked dazed and confused, her lips rosy and swollen. I dragged the elastic from her hair, finger-combing it out so it fell around her perfect, naked tits. Then I seized the bunched fabric and tore it right down the center.

We both gasped at the same time, her more from the shock of the rendering of the fabric. I sucked in a breath and the sight of a very bare pussy under the sheer, white material of her panties. Holy fuck. She'd gotten waxed, smooth...

Jade was suddenly sitting where I'd been, her back against the seat, her legs spread as I tossed them over my shoulders and shoved my face into her core. Inhaling her delicious scent, I ruined yet another piece of clothing in my desperation to taste her.

A long, slow lick from bottom to the top had her squirming, her hands once again clutching my head, and she was begging for more.

"More what, Jade?" I urged, "Of this?" Another long lick, then a quick little bite on her clit. She jerked as though shocked.

"Yes. More of yo—your mouth on—oh, yes!"

I did as I was told, tongue fucking her until she was screaming. "You're fucking soaked. I want you to come on my tongue, sweetheart. I want to taste it." I sucked on her clit a couple more times, then slid my tongue inside to touch the little spot that sent her spiraling out of control.

I was about to come all over the floor of the fucking car, so I snatched her up and switched places with her again. As soon as she was on her knees, I unzipped and freed my cock with a wince as it bounced painfully off of my stomach. I was so hard, my dick was leaking out pre-come from the red, angry tip.

Jade stared at it hungrily and I groaned. "Now, sweetheart. Take it in your mouth—oh, fuck." I couldn't finish the command because she grasped the base of my cock and sucked it deep, making my eyes roll to the back of my head. Her movements were the tiniest bit unsure, just as they were the first time she took me on her knees. I loved the idea of her not having a lot of experience doing this before me. Fuck if that didn't make it one hundred times hotter.

I threaded my fingers through her hair on either side of her head and held her close so I could pump into her mouth. "Keep your pretty lips closed around it, Jade. Good—ooooh—yeah, take more. I want to watch every inch disappear down your throat, sweetheart. Mmm, yes, that's fan-fucking-tastic."

She moaned as I spoke, the words adding to her own arousal, and I could tell she was enjoying this as much as I was. The thought of my woman getting off on sucking my cock was like a match to gasoline. My eyes slid closed and I began pumping up into her mouth, guiding her head as it bobbed up and down. "Suck it hard, sweetheart. Oh, fuck yeah."

I cracked my eyes open, wanting to watch my length disappear into her mouth and saw her hand creeping down toward her pussy. "No!" I barked and wrenched her away from me, startling her. I gripped her under the arms and dragged her up into my lap. "That pussy belongs to me, Jade," I snarled. "It's mine and only mine. If you need relief, pleasure, you ask me. I will be the one to give it to you. Is that clear?"

Jade blinked at me for a second, but it seemed to sink in and she smirked at me. "You own my pussy, Lucas?"

I made a strangled sound in the affirmative.

She leaned forward until our lips were a breath away, her gem colored eyes staring straight into my brown ones.

"Prove it."

My mouth crashed onto hers and I jerked her up before slamming her down on my cock, both of us rearing back and our lips separating as we cried out at the intense feeling. I rested against the seat and gripped her waist, watching as I started pounding up into her tight, hot, little pussy. Her big, beautiful tits bounced heavily as she rode me, her creamy white skin turning rosy with the flush of desire and need. Her hands landed on my shoulders, helping her to keep her balance as she met my every thrust, her head thrown back, lusty sounds of pleasure torn from her throat.

She was so fucking incredible and every time we were together it was more amazing than the last. I didn't know what that said for our life expectancy because if it got any better, it was liable to kill us. Who the fuck cared, anyway. What a way to go.

"Lucas, I'm almost—harder, babe! Harder!"

*Yes, ma'am.*

"Sit up on your knees on the seat, sweetheart," I commanded, "and spread your legs as wide as you can. Keep holding on to me for support."

She followed my instructions unquestioningly, trusting me to take care of her. Once she was in place, I widened my legs to keep her open and shifted her over me so she was slightly more forward over my groin.

In this position, every upward thrust had my cock angled to hit her g-spot. Moving my hands from her hips, I squeezed her ass in my palms and planted my feet flat on the ground. Using every bit of leverage, I began thrusting hard and fast, my pelvis slamming into her pussy, my balls slapping her ass and her cries became frantic, pleading for me to make her come.

"You wanted harder, sweetheart. I wanted deeper. Squeeze me, Jade. Don't let my cock go. You're so wet, I don't want to slide out. Hold on to me." The suctioning in her pussy grew and it was getting harder to drag my cock back out so I could dive back in. "Fuck, yeah! That's it, sweetheart. A little more."

I held off letting her go until I felt my balls draw up. A slow burn started at the base of my spine and spread quickly throughout my body. Gripping the cheeks of her ass so hard, I was sure I'd leave bruises, I parted the globes and one long middle finger rimmed the puckered little hole. She jolted and her eyes whipped open to stare at me in surprise, but I kept pushing forward. Literally.

"Trust me, sweetheart."

Eyes locked, on my next thrust, I dipped the tip of the finger inside and the muscles contracted, her pussy walls clamped down on my cock, and we came together with a shout.

Waves and waves of ecstasy crashed over me, hard jets of hot semen splashing inside her. Our bodies were shuddering with slowly abating convulsions, our lungs struggling to catch oxygen.

There was nothing, not the sun, the moon, or the stars, nothing as beautiful as Jade when she came. And, knowing I'm the man who put that look on her face, the *only* man who ever will again, it set off a second, smaller orgasm.

Jade slumped forward, collapsing on me, and my arms automatically went around her, gathering her close. I buried my face in her hair and took a long, slow breath. This was mine, for the rest of my life. Mine. And, nobody was going to convince me otherwise. I had enough wealth to start hundreds of new companies. If keeping Jade meant I lost the company I built with my dad, then so be it.

## Chapter 11

### Jade

After my morning ritual of puking and brushing my teeth, I left Lucas sleeping soundly in bed. He looked all rumpled and sexy, and I badly wanted to climb back in with him. I needed some ginger herbal tea and toast more than I yearned to feel the warmth of his arms wrapped around me again. I padded into the kitchen, giggling about the whole barefoot and pregnant thing as I puttered around. The laughter quickly died when I grabbed the paper from the counter. One of the cleaning staff Lucas had hired must have left it there for him to read over breakfast. Looking at the picture of the two of us staring up at me from the society pages, I was relieved to have beaten him down here.

The picture had been taken when he was helping me into the limousine. His hand had slipped from my lower back to the curve of my ass right when the photographer had snapped it. As if that wasn't bad enough, the look in his eyes was beyond heated. It reminded me of a wild animal who'd caught sight of its prey, and there was no mistaking who he was stalking—*his step-sister*, as the headline proclaimed in bold print.

"I can't seem to catch a break," I mumbled, dropping my head onto the cool granite of the countertop.

"Whatever it is, it can't be that bad, sweetheart," Lucas murmured in my ear, wrapping his body around me and pressing mine against the cabinets. "Not when my morning is starting off with the sight of you bent over like this."

My fist clenched and the crinkling of the newspaper caught his attention. He took a step backwards and slid the paper away from me, smoothing the wrinkles out as he read the article. I swiveled around, picking up my tea and sipping it while I watched him, wanting to see his reaction. His eyes were grave when they met mine once he was done. "Looks like the cat might be out of the bag. I better contact the company's head of public relations, fill her in on the situation and see how she thinks we should handle it."

He didn't look too upset, which surprised me considering what he'd told me about keeping our relationship quiet just the other day. It gave me hope for our future as a couple, but I didn't like being called a situation. I sure as heck didn't appreciate someone else getting to decide how, if, and when we talked about our relationship.

"I'll give you five days, Lucas."

"For what, sweetheart?" he asked distractedly, staring down at his cell phone while he typed out a message.

"Five days to figure out how you're going to *handle the situation*." I practically spit the words out. "I'm giving you five days to decide exactly how important I am to you."

My explanation certainly captured his attention, and his anger too, judging by the hint of fury in his eyes. "And what exactly happens after then?"

"I refuse to be your dirty secret. My mom was married to your dad one day before they died. We weren't raised together. Heck, we didn't even know each other when we first met, when we created a life together." My hand curled around my stomach protectively. "I'm not ashamed of what happened between us, of my feelings for you. For six weeks, I knew what it felt like to miss you. I like having you back in my life. More than like it, even."

I took a step closer to him, resting my hand on his chest while I stared up into his eyes. "I'm falling for you, Lucas. So hard and fast that I'm already half-in-love with you. Maybe even all the way."

His eyes lit with male satisfaction at my admission. "You have to know I I—"

I pressed my finger to his lips, stopping the flow of words. "Not like this." I shook my head emphatically, tears welling in my eyes. Stupid hormones. "Not right now. I want you to take these five days and really think about what you want. It can't be a knee-jerk reaction to the thought of losing me or the baby. And while you're thinking, you have to know I'd never keep you from him or her. Your decision needs to be about where you see our relationship going. Just the two of us, as a couple."

"Dammit, Jade, you're not being fair."

"I'm sorry," I murmured softly. "But I don't have time to worry about fair. I'm carrying your baby and I have my debut show to get ready for in five days. Once it's over, I'll be ready to hear what you have to say. Until then, I'll keep my lips shut to the press if anyone happens to call me. I won't be easy to find, though, since I'll be busy at the gallery."

"Too busy to spend time with me?" Disappointment was clear in his tone, and there might even have been a hint of hurt there too.

"I'll be home each night," I sighed. "In your bed, if that's where you want me."

"Then I guess we have a deal. Five days from today, the minute your art show is over, you'll have an answer," he gritted out, swooping down to claim my mouth in a brutal kiss. "In the meantime, your ass better be in my bed each night. Or else."

My knees buckled when he strode out of the room, and I moved over to the padded seat in front of the picture window and dropped down onto it. I'd snagged my phone off the counter on my way across the room and typed out a 911 text to my best friend. We'd been playing phone tag ever since I'd found out Lucas was my step-brother and I was pregnant with his baby. I'd had too much going on to worry about not connecting with her, but now it was urgent I spoke with her. I needed my bestie, she was the only person in the world who could possibly understand what I was going through. Lucky for me it only took about a minute before my phone rang with her call.

"Are you okay?" Bailey whispered frantically. I heard the rustling of fabric and realized I'd probably pulled her out of bed.

"Crap! I'm sorry," I apologized. "I didn't stop to think you might still be in bed."

"Don't worry about it. My sleep schedule is all messed up. I was just taking a little nap while a miracle was happening in the nursery. Jack and Julia are both down for an early morning nap."

"This can wait while you catch up on your sleep." It really couldn't wait long, but I felt like I should offer since she was a sleep-deprived mom with two three-month-olds.

"Shut up," she practically growled. "Well, not really. You know what I mean. You would never have sent me our emergency code unless it was urgent. So spill the beans. Now."

Spill them I did. I let her know about everything that had happened since we last spoke a week and a half ago. About Lucas being my step-brother, the pregnancy, and my feelings for him. I didn't spare a single detail, well except for a few about our sex life.

"Whoa!" She whistled once I was finally done. "It sounds like you found yourself in one hell of a situation, Jade."

"That's the understatement of the year," I groaned.

"How about I give you the same advice you gave me back when I came home to pack up my mom's house?"

I thought back to our dinner that night and laughed softly. "This is entirely different, Bailey. I told you to give him a chance, because from everything you'd told me about him, I knew he wanted you forever. You assumed Wyatt didn't want a relationship with you when he really did, but *Lucas* was the one to walk away from *me* after he accused me of horrible things. And even after we moved past all of that, he still said he wanted to keep our relationship a secret."

"But not forever," she pointed out gently. "Just until he figured out a way to protect his company, his father's legacy. Your child's future."

"Well, crap," I mumbled. "When you put it that way, I guess I can understand it a little better."

"And from everything you told me, it sounds like he's crazy about you."

"Do you really think so?" I cried.

"Yeah, Jade. I really do."

The night had been a rousing success. Almost all of my paintings had a sold sign underneath them. The prices listed by the gallery owner had been astronomical, and I couldn't believe how much I'd earned with my art. All in one night. I should have been over the moon happy, but all I could think about was the conversation I was about to have with Lucas. He'd hired a limousine for us again, but the ride home from the gallery was so different from the one back from L'étang. The only contact between the two of us was his hand clenched around mine as we rode in silence.

The last five days had passed much as our first few living together had, except I wasn't home as much because I was busy working on the final touches for my show. Lucas woke me up every morning with a cup of my tea and a couple slices of dry toast. He had lunch delivered to me each day, and dinner waiting at home at night. Not a single night had passed without us making love, and I'd slept soundly in his arms afterward. It was all perfect—except for my ultimatum hanging over us like a dark cloud.

Lucas took me at my word, and we hadn't spoken of it. I hadn't told him I loved him again, and he hadn't shared with me how he felt. I had no idea what he had decided, and the suspense was killing me. By the time the limo pulled into the drive, my stomach was twisted in knots. I didn't notice the driver had parked in front of the garage instead of the front door until Lucas helped me from the car. Lights flickered in the windows of the second story apartment. Lucas helped me up the stairs and I gasped when he swung the door open and I realized it was candles causing the glow.

Rose petals were scattered on the floor, and when I glanced up at the skylights, I saw twinkling stars in the night sky. The stage had definitely been set for romance, but I couldn't figure out why we were here instead of in the main house. As though Lucas had read my mind, he flipped the light switch on the wall and my question was answered.

"A studio?" I gasped, twirling around the room and gawking at all the equipment he'd had brought in. "You turned the apartment into a studio for me?"

"I did," he confirmed, dropping down to one knee in front of me. "My wife is an artist. She needed a studio so she can share her incredible talent with the world. It's why I had my assistant working on it since the morning after I found out about the pregnancy."

*The morning after...* he'd been working on this since before my ultimatum. I didn't realize how important it was to me until this very moment.

"I'm not your wife yet."

He reached into his pocket and pulled out a flawless diamond ring. "In my heart you are, Jade. I haven't been able to forget about you since the moment we met. If I hadn't allowed past experiences to cloud my better judgment, I never would have let you go and you'd already have my ring on your finger. I love you," he paused to look down at the ring, moving it to the tip of my finger. "And I want the world to know you're mine. Will you marry me?"

The studio, gorgeous diamond ring, and proposal, it was more than I'd ever dreamt about how this conversation would go. It looked like Lucas had used every minute I'd given him to set out to prove how he felt about me. There was only one possible answer I could give. "Yes."

## *Epilogue*

## LUCAS

"Well, Mr. and Mrs. St. James, it looks like a girl this time," the doctor informed us with a smile before wiping Jade's stomach and lowering the hem of her maternity top. "Do you have a name picked out?"

"Ruby!"

Shit. My hand wasn't fast enough to cover the mouth of my three-year-old son before he shouted the name. He twisted in my arms and beamed at me before his face fell and his own two chubby, little hands slapped over his mouth.

"I forgot, Daddy," he muffled through his fingers.

I winked at him and kissed the tip of his nose, "It's okay buddy. You did great." It was my own fault for trusting a toddler with a secret.

"Her name is what?" Jade asked, raising a quizzical brow in my direction. Her tone clearly indicated she wasn't happy.

I cleared my throat and shifted uncomfortably, weighing my options on how to handle this situation. I wasn't budging on my baby girl's name, so I decided to go with standing firm.

"You picked out Jonathan's name and we agreed I'd get to pick our next baby's name. I choose Ruby."

Jade's eyes narrowed as she glared at me, but any response was cut off by the doctor.

"What a lovely name."

I grinned triumphantly at Jade, who rolled her eyes.

"Everything looks great," the doctor continued, "so I'll see you back here for your next appointment on schedule."

She stood, shook our hands, and waved at Jonathan before leaving the room.

He returned the gesture enthusiastically. "Thanks for the Ruby!" he called after her, making me chuckle. Then he turned to me and took my breath away with one of his giant, baby boy smiles. "I'm hungry. So Ruby must be hungry. Let's feed Ruby!"

Apparently, now that the cat was out of the bag, my son was unintentionally determined to get me in trouble by calling the baby Ruby as many times as possible.

Jade patted her rounded belly and then his little one. "Yep, both my little babies want some dinner." Then she grabbed my ass and whispered to me, "We'll discuss this after peanut is in bed."

*Bed. Perfect idea.* I smiled my most charming, panty-melting grin, and agreed. The heat in her eyes shifted a little from anger to lust and I mentally gave myself a pat on the back for the plan I'd suddenly concocted.

I brushed a kiss across the soft skin of Jonathan's forehead and pulled his giraffe covered blanket up to his chin. Padding out into the hall, I shut the door silently, before making my way to our bedroom.

I'd received a work call during dinner and had to excuse myself. Our company had taken a pretty direct hit when the picture of us had been splashed across the papers. Then, someone inside my organization leaked my plans for the restructure to the board and they went apeshit. Most of them had walked, taking all of our bigger clients with them.

My first instinct had been to scramble and save the crumbling empire, but during a conversation with Jade, she asked me what it was my father and I loved about the company. Mulling over my answer, I realized it was because he and I had built and developed the product together.

My father had left all of the patents to me in his will. So, I dissolved the company and started a research facility instead. I returned to where I belonged, in the lab, improving the technology instead of peddling it. After two years, we had a break through and we were approached with a government contract. I hired a CEO, to run the business side of things, and continued to keep being "the mad scientist," as Jade liked to call me. I liked to think my dad would be happy with where my career had taken me, and even more so with the state of my personal life.

When I finished my call, Jade had already put our son to bed and I knew she'd planned to take a bath. Our room was still and empty when I entered it, but there was light coming from under the bathroom door. Assuming she was still soaking in the tub, I hurried to set everything as I wanted it in order to seduce my wife into agreeing to whatever I wanted. I had a decent track record of making her scream yes when something was important to me.

I set the baby monitor on the dresser, put out candles and soft music, turned down the bed, and retrieved my secret weapon from the kitchen, setting it on the table next to the bed. After everything was just right, I changed into a pair of pajama pants and knocked on the bathroom door.

"Sweetheart?"

"I'm about done in here, Lucas. I'll be out in a minute."

She sounded relaxed instead of angry. *Excellent.*

I walked back to the bed and was about to open my package when I heard the door creak. Turning around, I stumbled back at the overwhelming sight in front of me.

Jade was wearing a white, lacy thong, glittery white pasties, thigh highs, and silver "fuck me" heels. She placed a hand high up on either side of the door jam, her hip popped out, and her head cocked to the side so her long, platinum hear cascaded down the side of her body. The rounded bump of her stomach only added to the appeal of her look. She smiled seductively and my balls tightened. *Relax boys.*

"You look amazing, sweetheart," I rasped as I wandered toward her.

Her green eyes swept down over her outfit pensively. "You don't think I look like a stripper?"

I choked out a laugh at her comment, remembering how I'd assumed she was an exotic dancer the first time we met because of her looks and her name.

"Was that the look you were going for?" I asked as I stopped right in front of her.

She shimmied a little as she brushed past me, the heavy globes of her tits bouncing. Stopping, she looked back over her shoulder, gazing at me through lowered lashes.

"Would you like a private dance, Mr. St. James?"

I smiled and made my way to a small couch in the sitting area, getting settled before gesturing for her to go ahead.

I knew her game, and I was determined to win, but I couldn't help testing the limits of my control by letting her play her hand a little longer. She began to move with the music, slow and sensual, her body like liquid sex.

I was tempted to check for drool, but I managed to keep my cool, barely. "If this is a ploy to get me to change my mind about the name Ruby, you can forget it, wife," I growled. Her eyes widened innocently and it was so fucking sexy, I snapped.

I stalked toward her and carefully tossed her on the bed. After stripping us both, I wasted no time thrusting inside her. We moaned in unison as heat rushed between us, getting hotter with every drive of my cock into her tight pussy.

"This doesn't mean you've won, sweetheart," I whispered in her ear before nipping at the lobe, feeling her shiver.

My hands slid up her arms to her wrists, holding them above her head and my head dipped to taste her nipples. Jade's tits were her downfall when she was pregnant. I'd finally completed my experiment and had discovered that I could, in fact, make her come just from playing with her nipples.

Her knees bent and she squeezed my hips between her thighs, the walls of her pussy attempting to milk my orgasm from me before I was ready. Leaving her wrists in one hand, I brought the other down to spank her ass as I bit lightly on one little peak. She gasped and arched, forcing me even deeper.

"Oh, fuck, yes!" I grunted, picking up speed. Damn it. I was losing every shred of control. But, I wouldn't concede victory, not yet.

My hand slipped between us to pet her swollen little clit as my mouth descended on hers. After a thorough kiss, I inclined my head so my mouth brushed her ear when I spoke. "I love you," I cooed as I pinched her clit and thrust hard.

Any thoughts of being the victor went flying when she exploded around me and it set off my own orgasm. I shouted her name and pumped into her with every shockwave as they washed over me.

Later, after we'd returned to earth, I leaned against the headboard with Jade on my lap, feeding her spoonfuls of the chocolate mousse I'd originally brought up to torture her with.

"I named Jonathan after you and your father, Lucas Jonathan St. James!" she argued as we continued our debate about names.

"And, I want to name my baby girl, Ruby, like her mother, Jade, because you are both my most precious gems," I purred.

Cheesy, yes. And yet, I waited, and then I heard it, the little sniff. I grinned widely, certain I'd won.

"Lucas?" She asked softly.

"Hmmm?"

"Did you picture me in an outfit like the one from tonight when we first met?"

I shrugged, scooping out the last of the dessert and feeding it to her. "I suppose a picture of something like it flashed in my head when I heard your name."

She swallowed and leaned against me, dropping her head back to meet my eyes. "And what do you suppose other men will picture when they look at your daughter, who will most likely look a lot like me, and are introduced to Ruby St. James."

I froze. Well, fuck.

She smiled with smug satisfaction at the look on my face. "I win."

I grumbled but had no argument.

"Maybe we'll use it for her middle name."

Jade laughed heartily and patted the side of my face sympathetically.

"Babe, it doesn't really matter what her name is, if she looks much like me, they'll be picturing it anyway."

The absolute and complete horror I felt at the moment must have been clear on my face because Jade scrambled to her knees and faced me.

"Are you okay? What's wrong?"

"Fuck, no," I croaked. "No girls. Tell the doctor to change it. We can only have boys."

Jade's concern quickly dissolved into another fit of laughter and I glared at her.

"You sound just like Bailey's husband, Wyatt." She rolled her eyes and started clearing things off of the bed while I calmed down.

She urged me to slip down so I was laying on my back and she curled herself into me, yawning.

"I mean it, Jade. After this one, boys only."

She sighed. "Okay, Lucas. But that means no more getting pregnant, so we won't be having sex anymore."

"What the fuck?" I roared, jackknifing up and knocking Jade off of my chest.

She fell into a puddle of giggles at my reaction.

"Oh, babe. You should see the look on our face."

I did not find her joke the least bit funny. "It's not something you joke about, Jade."

"Relax, lover boy," she said as she snuggled into her pillow.

My eyes narrowed as I stared at her voluptuous body. I felt the overwhelming need to prove it was no joking matter.

Tossing her pillow and blanket away, I attacked her with the sole purpose of making sure she would never ever, even consider the idea of being deprived of the pleasure I could bring her.

By the time I was done, we both collapsed on the bed, sweaty, practically comatose.

"You're right," she panted. "I couldn't live without it."

"Damn fucking straight," I grunted.

"You'll just have to wear a condom," she said and started giggling again.

I snorted, "Nothing between us, sweetheart." I summoned the rest of my strength to smack her sweet little ass before wrapping myself around her. Snuggling closer, one hand resting possessively on her tummy, I sighed and buried my face in her neck.

I'd go hunting for a new name in the morning. I was determined to find one that told the world she was my treasure, just like her mother.

# Bonus Scene: Happy Anniversary

## LUCAS

"Happy anniversary, sweetheart," I whispered, trailing the petals of a soft, pink rose over her cheek, down and across her collarbone.

Jade's eyes fluttered and she slowly began to wake, a beautiful smile gracing her face. With a little tug on the sheet, her generous tits were bare for me to feast my eyes on. I continued to slide the rose along her skin and over her nipples, going rock fucking hard at the sound of her gasp. An amazing feat, considering how stiff my cock had already been.

Unable to stop myself, I replaced the rose with my mouth, sucking and licking her nipples as they hardened into peaks. "Lucas!" Jade's cry had all of my romantic plans flying out of the window. Ripping the sheet fully away, I freed my cock from my boxers and settled between Jade's legs. I took her mouth in a deep kiss as I thrust deep inside her.

"Oh fuck, baby! I had you last night. How come I feel so desperate to fuck you right now?"

"Lucas, stop talking about it and do it," she demanded.

"Anything you want, sweetheart." I fucked her rough and hard, the headboard banging against the wall.

"Lucas!" she hissed. "The kids."

"Staying at a friend's house," I growled, pounding into her sweet pussy. "There's nobody to hear you scream but me, baby. Now, let me hear everything I do to you."

She moaned and lifted her hips eagerly to meet my thrusts. "Jade!" I snapped.

"I can't—I'm so used to—Oh, Lucas! Oh yes! Harder!"

"Good girl," I grunted. Her cries turned to delicious screams until she arched her back and stiffened, then broke into a million pieces. I followed after, roaring her name as I poured my orgasm into her.

"So, no kids today, huh?" Jade asked, a sly edge to her tone as she panted, her heart rate beginning to return to normal.

I leaned down and nibbled her ear before telling her, "No kids all weekend, sweetheart. So, don't expect to leave this bed much or be able to walk when you do."

She sighed a sound of contentment, "Is this my anniversary present?"

I rolled my eyes. "Of course not, it's mine."

Jade laughed. "Figures. What do I get then?"

I grinned. "Another baby." She snorted and looked at me like I was crazy. I stared back at her, perfectly serious.

"Lucas, that's another present for you. One I wasn't aware I was giving you."

Caressing the side of her face, I moved my hand over to play with her earlobe. "Maybe it's the new diamonds in your ears." She gasped, and her hands flew up to touch the three-carat diamond studs I'd managed to get into her ears without waking her. As well as her second present. I touched the matching solitaire, lying just above the valley of her tits. "Or perhaps the one hanging around your neck."

Jade shoved me off of her and ran to the mirror. "Holy shit! They're freaking huge, Lucas!" She returned to the bed, a stunned look still lingering on her face. Climbing on the bed, she crawled over to me (Yep. The sight had my cock wound so tight, I was in pain) and kissed me softly.

"Thank you. They're beautiful."

"Not nearly as beautiful as you." I palmed her tits. "Now about my presents..."

I trailed off when she straddled me, wiggling over my erection. "We can practice making a baby. How about that?" I pouted, and she rolled her eyes. "You'll get your official present in seven months, you big baby."

I felt my eyes become round as saucers and a massive smile split my face. "You're right, we should practice for the next one."

"The next one?" she shrieked.

I didn't give her a chance to think about my words, instead, keeping her mind fully engaged in orgasm after orgasm.

Happy anniversary, indeed.

# Baby, Don't Go

Yeah, Baby 3

## FIONA DAVENPORT

# Chapter 1

## JACK

"Hey, Ellie!" I yelled as I jogged down the sterile halls of the hospital. A white lab coat and dark brown ponytail had just disappeared around the corner. As I reached the turn, I rammed into said lab coat and ponytail, knocking us both to the ground. I caught her as we fell, so that she landed on top of me. Soft tits were pressed against my chest, wisps of straight, toffee-colored hair tickled my chin, and a sweet, elfin face grinned at me, while her hazel eyes danced with amusement.

"You're pretty clumsy for a surgeon, honey," she laughed, then lightly smacked my shoulder. "And, would you stop calling me Ellie?"

The endearment brought warmth to my chest and her laugh started a buzz in the general area of my dick. I shoved both feelings away. Ellison Reed was my friend. In fact, since my best friend had gone and knocked up, then married my sister, Ellie (no, I wouldn't stop calling her that) had basically taken his place.

She jumped to her feet and I followed, my own grin splitting my face. "I don't know what you're talking about, Dr. Reed. You plowed into me.

Ellison snorted, "You wish."

Yes. I did wish, but I wasn't about to admit it aloud. I raised a single eyebrow. "You think so?"

She shook her head. "Well, since your blow-up girlfriend deflated..."

I tweaked her nose. "Funny, funny girl."

Winking at me, she curtseyed. "Thank you."

*Damn, she was adorable.* Or, you know, cute. Like a friend. "Alright, Dr. Comedienne, I have a surgery in half an hour, but I wanted to see if we were still on for movie night at my place."

"Yep. My last case should be done by five, so I'll grab a shower and pick up Chinese on the way. I should be there by six."

"Great. And none of that all vegetable crap you got last time. I'm a growing boy, I need meat, woman!" Her short ponytail was swinging and I couldn't resist tugging it before I walked away, her laughter following me, bringing back those damn tingles.

Ellison and I had worked together on and off over the last two years. She was a general pediatric surgeon and when her patients needed a specialist in pediatric vascular surgery, she usually requested me. However, a few months ago, we ran into a tough case and ended up working long hours together. We began to realize we had a lot in common, a love of crappy horror movies, Thai food, eighties music, and baseball. When Wyatt, had to cancel a baseball game with me, I invited Ellison. From there, things took off and we'd been inseparable ever since.

I'd always been attracted to her, but the friendship we'd developed was important to me and I decided never to cross the line out of the "friend zone." Friday nights became movie night for us most weeks and I was looking forward to unwinding with her, a cold beer, and a shitty B-list horror film.

My afternoon was spent with a tough case, and by the time the surgery was done, I was strung tight with stress and worry.

"I want updates every hour for the next four hours," I told my nurse as I finished writing Heather's orders. She was only six years old and in critical condition. "Then I want another update every four hours from then on."

"No problem, Dr. Halston." She finished hooking up Heather's IV and followed me from the small room in the ICU, both of us stopping at the nurse's station to drop off paperwork.

I changed into street clothes in the locker room and tossed my scrubs in a laundry bin on my way out the door. Entering the employee-parking garage, I strolled over to my Mercedes convertible and popped the remote lock. Getting in, I put down the top and drove out into the balmy, summer evening. On the way home, I stopped by the store for beer and a carton of Moose Tracks, Ellison's favorite ice cream. When I arrived at my house, I pulled into the four-car garage and parked next to my Ducati. Taking everything inside, I put the groceries away and hopped in the shower, washing away the grime and some of the stress from the day. Afterwards, I dressed in an old pair of comfy jeans and a grey T-shirt, but stayed barefoot, enjoying the feel of my soft, plush carpet on my feet.

I pulled my comforter off of the bed and took it to the couch, knowing Ellie would get cold and ask me for it eventually anyway, and tossed it onto one of the couches in my theater room. I checked my phone for an update on my patient and was pleased to know she was improving. When the doorbell rang, I walked down the hall and into my large entryway, to the front door and twisted the handle. Opening it, I found Ellison holding plastic bags in one hand and munching on an egg roll with the other. Her plump lips closed around the cylindrical food and I fought a groan as I suddenly pictured those plump lips around a similarly shaped part of my body. *You need to get laid, dude.* Clearly, six months of celibacy had put my fucking hormones into overdrive. It didn't help matters to see her wearing yoga pants that molded to her very fine legs and ass, and a large T-shirt that hung off one shoulder, revealing a bright purple bra strap.

"That better not be my egg roll," I growled playfully. Her eyes widened with innocent shock as she took another bite.

"You wanted one?" She popped the last of the greasy treat into her mouth and chewed slowly. I rolled my eyes and stood back, allowing her to enter.

"I saved you all of the crab rangoons, though," she tossed over her shoulder.

I felt my face screw up in a disgusted grimace, I hated seafood. "Hardy har, Ellie. Now, give me my food."

She set the bags on the table while I grabbed plates and silverware, bringing them over to her. We dished up our food, I grumbled over the vegetable fried rice and lo mein, and then we each grabbed a beer and headed for my theater room, settling on a couch to watch our movie. Ellie finished off two plates of food and I wondered, not for the first time, where she put all of it. She was barely five foot three and no more than one hundred and ten pounds, soaking wet. An image I've pictured a million times. I grabbed our plates, taking them to the kitchen and returning to find she'd taken over my couch. As usual.

She was wrapped up in the blanket I'd left for her and I lifted her mummified feet, so I could sit back on my end of the couch and let them drop into my lap. They were dangerously close to my cock and he had definitely taken notice. I focused on the movie, determined to forget about her sexy body and the proximity of her cute little feet to my budding erection. At one point, she ran a toe up her opposite leg, likely scratching it, but it was sexy as hell, and I had to clench my fists in order to keep from following the path of her foot with my hands. Then she shifted and when she brushed against my hard as fuck cock, I almost came in my pants right then and there. If she noticed the bulge in my crotch, she didn't mention it and I wasn't going to bring it up. All in all, it was fucking agony.

I managed to get through it, but when the credits started to roll, I jumped up, almost knocking her to the ground.

"Hey!" she yelped as she caught herself.

"Sorry, I need some...um...ice cream!" I hurried to the kitchen and opened the freezer, basking in the cool air. I dished up the bowls and returned to the living room, handing hers over and taking a seat in my black, leather recliner.

"Ready for the sequel?" I asked as I cued up the DVR.

She licked her spoon and let out a tiny little moan of delight. *Fuck!* Ok, stupid choice of words.

"Sure. Although, I'm not sure I'll be able to stay for it all."

I glanced at her in surprise. "You know you can crash here if it gets too late or if you want to have a couple of beers."

She nodded absentmindedly, continuing to dig into her ice cream, searching out the little peanut butter cups. "Yeah, I know. It's not that. I have an early date tomorrow."

Something inside me started to burn, an irrational anger building. Her *date* was cutting into my time with her, the bastard.

"What kind of a date happens on Saturday morning?" I muttered rhetorically.

"He's taking me horseback riding and wants to get an early start before it gets really hot." She didn't seem particularly enthusiastic about the date and it soothed a little of my ire. Why was I mad? What the fuck was wrong with me? I was being ridiculous.

"Sounds like he's a pretentious snob, showing off."

Ellison laughed at my comment, giving me a dry look. "Excuse me, but don't you own horses, Jack?"

"That's different," I huffed. "We're friends. I'd take you riding if you wanted to go. But, taking a woman horseback riding for a first date? What a tool."

It was Ellison's turn to roll her eyes and mutter, "What crawled up your ass tonight?"

"Nothing. I just think you shouldn't waste your time with losers and this guy is obviously trying to get in your pants by throwing his money in your face."

"What? Jack, seriously, what is wrong with you tonight?" Ellison stood and left the room. I followed at a slow pace, confused by my own behavior and having lost my appetite. I found her in the kitchen, loading all of our dishes into the dishwasher.

"I'm sorry," I mumbled. "Bad day, I guess."

She sighed. "Yeah. I'm going to head out."

I felt something akin to panic creeping into my chest. I couldn't let her walk out the door, because it would mean she'd be going on a date tomorrow morning. I couldn't let it happen, I just couldn't. I was stunned at my reaction and didn't know what to make of it. Before I was able to form a response, Ellison had left the room. I trotted to the entryway to find her grabbing her keys and cell phone from the glass bowl on the little marble table by the coat closet.

I stood there, watching, my arms hanging at my sides, not knowing what to do or say. She glanced at me with a half-smile as she slipped on her flip-flops and headed to the door.

I joined her and put my hand on it to keep it closed. "I'll see you Sunday for breakfast?" I asked tentatively.

"Oh, sorry. I forgot to tell you, he's taking me to a cabin by a lake for the night. That's why we want to get on the trail before the heat is unbearable."

"Your—um," I croaked as something began to choke me. "Your date is overnight? As in spending the night with him, in the cabin, alone?"

Ellison looked at me curiously. "Yes."

*No. No fucking way in hell was that happening.*

The tightness in my chest and throat snapped and a rush of adrenaline, lust, and uncontrollable need rushed through my body as though a dam had broken. My hand cupped the back of her neck, the other grasping her waist, and pulled her flush against my body, my mouth slamming down over hers.

# Chapter 2

## Ellison

I gasped in surprise as Jack's tongue slid inside my mouth. It tangled with mine as he devoured me, kissing me the way I'd always assumed he would on the rare occasions I allowed my thoughts to wander in that direction. Jack Halston was a sexy devil. I'd known it from the first moment I'd laid eyes on him, just as every woman did. At six foot two, with a toned body that showed he worked out during his off hours, dark hair that looked like he'd just rolled out of bed, and chocolate brown eyes that always seemed to be smiling, he was impossible to miss. At first, I was happy for him to be my work flirt when our paths crossed on a shared case. We didn't see each other often enough for it to be awkward, and I enjoyed the little thrill I got from the way we bantered back and forth.

Flirting with Jack offered me a naughty distraction, but I knew nothing would ever come of it. Jack had a rule about not sleeping with anyone from the hospital, a fact long bemoaned by the vast majority of the female staff who would have given just about anything to make him break it. There was no way I'd be the one to make him throw his rulebook out the window. When our friendship deepened a few months ago, the slim chance I ever had of seeing Jack naked became even less likely because we went from being work peers to friends. If a guy like Jack didn't sleep with his co-workers, then he most definitely didn't screw any of his female friends. A fact I'd reminded myself of each time I'd woken up from dreams about all the things I'd do to him if I ever had the chance.

I wasn't about to waste an opportunity like this. Shoving away all thoughts of what might happen to our friendship if this went sideways, I dropped my keys and phone back down and reveled in the feel of his lips over mine.

"Fuck it," he groaned into my mouth. "I'm done playing the nice guy, trying to ignore how hard you make me because you're my friend and co-worker. How you've made it fucking impossible for me to even look at another woman without comparing her to you."

Wait? Had his recent dry spell been because of *me*? Because I could definitely lay the blame for mine at his feet. It was hard to find a guy who measured up to my dreams of Jack. I'd finally talked myself into accepting this date with a guy who'd asked me about a dozen times whenever I bumped into him at the gym. The only reason I'd said yes was because I figured that at some point, I'd have to hear about Jack's dates with another woman.

"I'm not letting you walk out this door, knowing you'll be with some douchebag this weekend. He doesn't get to touch what's mine," he growled, making my pussy quiver at the possessiveness in his tone.

"And what exactly do you consider to be yours?" Yeah, that was my raspy voice, taunting him with my question when we both knew what he meant. I couldn't help myself. He'd started this, and I wanted to make sure he damn well finished it.

He crowded me closer to the door, his hard chest pressed against mine while his big hands held my hips. My heart raced as his lips traced a path along my cheek and up to my ear. His breath was hot as he answered my question, his fingers tightening on me. "You're mine."

"Oh, yeah?" I breathed. "Prove it, honey."

"I fucking love it when you call me honey." His voice was dark and dangerous, with none of the teasing quality that was always there between us. "And I can't fucking wait to taste yours."

His lips on me sounded like a great plan. "Yes, please."

"Looking at your curves without being able to touch them was pure torture." His hand drifted up from my hip, along the curve of my waist and my side until it rested below one of my tits. My nipples pebbled as his thumb swept upwards. His other hand tightened on my hip, holding me firmly against his cock while his hips flexed and pressed his length against me. "See what you do to me? I'm a walking hard-on whenever you're near."

"Maybe we should do something about that," I murmured, running my hands down his back, his muscles bunching underneath my fingertips.

"Not until I get my taste of you."

He dropped to his knees, shoving my yoga pants and panties down my legs and ripping them and my flip-flops off my body. He widened my stance and without warning, two fingers plunged into me. His thumb stayed on my clit, rubbing in circles.

I moaned, riding his hand as his fingers worked in and out of me, staring down at his dark head as his body flexed with each thrust of his fingers. All coherent thought flew out of my brain when he leaned forward and replaced his thumb with his lips at my clit. Alternating between sucking and licking, he never stopped thrusting his two fingers into me.

"I'm so close," I cried out, my body tightening when he sucked my clit hard and bit down gently. Intense pleasure ripped through my body, my hips jerking against him. He yanked his fingers out of me and slid his tongue as deep as it would go, fucking me through my orgasm as I rode his face.

He stood, keeping one hand on my waist to steady me. I was dazed from my climax, my eyes unable to focus on the sight of him fumbling with his zipper to free his cock.

"Tell me you want me inside you." He didn't wait for my answer, his lips crashing against mine once again. I tasted myself on him, our flavors mixed together. "Please, Ellie," he whispered against my mouth.

"Yes." My answer turned into a gasp when his hands grabbed the back of my thighs to pick me up. My legs wrapped around his hips, lining us up perfectly. He drove inside in one powerful thrust, my back slamming against the door.

He dropped his forehead onto mine, his brown eyes appearing even darker with desire. My pussy squeezed in response to the possessive gleam in them. My brain might not be sure exactly what was happening between us, but my body seemed more than okay to go with the flow and enjoy the ride.

"This first time, I know I should be gentle. I'm sorry I can't be," he groaned, grinding his hips into me and driving his cock even deeper. "I've waited too long and want you too much, but I swear I'll make it good for you, my Ellie."

"It's more than good just like this," I promised. "Take me, honey."

"So fucking perfect." His voice was rough against my neck as I wrapped my arms around his shoulders and tried moving my hips. His hold on me tightened further, to the point I was going to have bruises in the morning. Marks I'd wear proudly as a reminder of our night together.

He withdrew and then plunged back inside. Over and over again while he held me immobile against the wall and fucked me. Slowly at first and then his rhythm sped up, pushing me closer to the edge. I gasped each time he pounded into me, my cries ringing out between us.

"Come for me," he growled. "I need to feel your tight pussy strangling my cock."

I flew apart, moaning loudly as my body convulsed around him. My pussy fluttered, my legs tightening on his hips, and my arms clenching around his neck. My orgasm was huge. I swore I saw stars.

"Hottest thing I've ever seen," he groaned. "Just seeing you like that is enough to make me come, too."

His body shuddered as he proved his words to be true. He came hot and hard, deep inside me as he trembled. His hips pushed deeper, driving him further inside while his come filled me up and spilled down my thighs.

"Fuck," he hissed. "You feel so damn good, Ellie."

He felt better than good inside me. Of course he did. It wasn't just because we fit together perfectly, almost like his cock had been made to fill me. Nope, it felt beyond amazing because we'd done something I'd never done before. Jack had taken me bare. Without protection of any kind because I wasn't on birth control, hadn't been since I was a teenager and discovered I didn't react to the hormones well. We were doctors, for fuck's sake. We both knew the risks better than most people, and yet the thought of telling him to use a condom hadn't crossed my mind. Not once. *What the heck was up with that?*

## Chapter 3

## JACK

I had dreamed of fucking Ellison so many times, woken up in a cold sweat, on the verge of coming night after night. It didn't even come close to the real thing. I could barely breathe. My heart was pounding so hard, and while I felt sated from the relief of finally having her, it also fed my obsession. My cock was still hard as a rock, gloved in the heat of her pussy.

My hands moved from her hips to her plump, luscious ass and I quickly walked her to the back of the house and into my bedroom, not once losing our connection. Lowering her gently to the bed, I slipped out, her little mewl of protest hardening my cock even further, despite having just emptied myself into her. I tore my T-shirt over my head and dropped my jeans and boxers to the floor before joining her on the bed again. I helped her lift her shirt up and off, tossing it randomly because my eyes were glued to her tits, watching the full globes encased in purple silk rise and fall as she panted with arousal.

My hands slid up her sides, over her flat belly, and up to cup her tits. They filled my palms perfectly and I squeezed them, almost breaking at the sound of Ellison moaning. I reached one hand beneath her back and popped the clasp. The bra loosened and her tits spilled out, her dark pink nipples large and erect, begging for my mouth.

"You're fucking gorgeous, Ellie," I rumbled before taking one peak in my mouth. They tasted sweet, and I licked and sucked them like a fucking lollipop until Ellison was writhing, her fisted hands clutching the covers.

I could feel the sticky come between us and I decided to live out the fantasy of my woman soaking wet. In more ways than one. "Let's shower, baby."

She glared at me and I grinned and kissed her. "I promise it'll be the best fucking shower you've ever had."

She raised a single eyebrow and my smile widened. "Yeah, I definitely meant it both ways."

She laughed and I pulled her up off the bed, lifting her in my arms, to carry her to the bathroom while she clung to me, arms and legs locked around my body. I settled her on the counter and stepped inside my spacious, marble shower, turning on the water and waiting for it to heat to the perfect temperature.

Then I returned to her and picked her up, her body once again wrapping itself around me. I stepped under the spray and she groaned in pleasure.

"Ellie, baby, you keep making noises like that and you'll find yourself being fucked up against a second wall tonight."

"Promise?" she asked, her voice whisper soft, bathing the shell of my ear in her warm breath. I was tempted, so tempted, but there was something else I wanted more.

I lathered up my hands and washed her from head to toe, my control severely tested when she did the same to me. After rinsing, I grasped her waist and pulled her soft body into me.

"Now," I mumbled against her skin as I kissed my way down her body, "about your honey." I lowered to my knees and gasped at the glistening pink pussy on display. Rivulets of water ran down her legs and I had to know if the wetness was all from the shower. I parted her folds and immediately gave her one long, slow lick.

The taste of honey burst on my tongue and I growled before attacking her pussy. My tongue and teeth went to work, building my Ellie up until she was crying out.

I added two fingers to the mix and she screamed my name as she shattered. I jumped to my feet, spun her around, placed her hands on the wall, and thrust up into her pussy which was still pulsing with her orgasm. "Fuck, baby. You feel so good." I pulled her hips out a little and tilted her pussy, driving deeper before she could come down off of the ledge, and she was coming again. "I want another one, Ellie. Come on, baby. Take me deep." I thrust in harder and harder until I wrung a third orgasm from her and finally allowed myself to come. It rocked my fucking world.

After we had managed to catch our breath, I ran a hand from her hip down to cup her pussy. I felt a thick wetness leaking out and coating my fingers. Bringing my hand from between her legs, I stared at it covered in come.

*What the fuck did I just do?*

I'd taken Ellie bare. Twice. *Son of a bitch!*

We'd have to talk about it, but I needed time to process this, so I didn't say anything yet. She seemed to be in a haze, exhausted and sated. I fucking loved the look on her face. It brought the warmth back to my chest. I rinsed both of us and shut the water off before stepping out onto the heated tile. Grabbing two towels, I wrapped one around my waist, then gently dried Ellie off. Lifting her into my arms, I carried her to my big bed and helped her slide under the covers, before going around to the other side, climbing in, and pulling her into my arms. Her head rested on my shoulder and she sighed, gliding her hand over my stomach and up to rest on my sternum.

Holding her close, I contemplated our circumstances. From a previous conversation, I knew she wasn't on any type of birth control because of adverse reactions she'd experienced. I hadn't intended to act on the chemistry between us, but now that I had, there was no fucking way I was going to let her go. I wanted this, having her in my bed every night, forever. I pictured her walking down a flower covered aisle in a white dress and felt nothing but need and want, whereas I expected to be in a panic. The image morphed into a picture of Ellison with a swollen belly, her smile bright, and I was infused with excitement.

This could actually be the silver bullet. I wanted a family, especially after spending time with my sister, her husband, and their twins. I'd begun to seriously consider settling down. After giving in to my body's craving for Ellie, I realized I definitely wanted those things, but only with her. A baby would cement our commitment to each other. She was mine and everyone would know it.

The more I thought about it, the idea grew until I was determined to make it happen. Fuck the condoms, if Ellie wasn't already pregnant, I'd make damn sure she was as soon as possible. Getting her moved in right away was the first step to tackle. Set on a course of action, I fell asleep with a smile on my face and dreamt of my perfect future.

The next morning, I woke slowly, contentment washing over me as I ran my hands down the soft flesh of my woman wrapped up in my arms. She stirred and I looked down to see her eyes flutter then widen as her head popped up, looking around with something akin to panic in them. I frowned, frustrated that she apparently wasn't feeling the same level of satisfaction at waking up with me. She slowly went up onto an elbow and twisted to meet my gaze. The panic had eased, but it had been replaced with wariness.

"Good morning, beautiful," I purred, the back of my hand running down her cheek before pushing her hair back behind her ear. My words seemed to melt some of the wariness away and the tension in her shoulders lessened. She smiled at me, almost shyly, and it was so adorable I had to kiss her. Putting my hands on her torso, I hauled her up to press my lips to hers.

My morning hard-on was suddenly hard as a baseball bat and I scowled when she pulled back. She smiled again and I softened at the sight, wondering if she would always have the same effect on me.

"Morning," she whispered. She shifted and I saw a tiny wince, worrying me.

"Are you sore, baby? I probably shouldn't have taken you so hard last night."

Her cheeks became a sweet shade of pink. "Um, a little." She winked at me. "That battering ram you call a dick is larger than I'm used to." She mock glared at me. "Don't let that go to your head, honey. You have a hard enough time getting through doors as it is."

I laughed and enveloped her in a hug. I fucking loved her—what? I was glad she couldn't see my face at the moment. I'm sure I looked like a deer in headlights. Holy fuck. When had it happened? I was so in love with her. I just needed to make her fall in love with me, too. There was no other option.

"Why don't you hop in the shower, baby? I'll make us some breakfast."

She pouted at me, and I chortled. "If I take a shower with you, you'll be even more sore."

With a quick peck on her lips, I scooted to the edge of the bed and stood. Grabbing my cell phone, I checked my messages for news about Heather as I rooted around for my boxers and picked up all of our scattered clothes, throwing them in the hamper.

"Hey!" Ellie protested. "I don't have any other clothes here, honey."

I opened a drawer and tossed a T-shirt and clean boxers at her. She caught them and frowned. "I can't go home in these."

I raised an eyebrow. "Who said you were leaving?"

"I need to go home," she huffed.

I didn't reply until I was almost out the door then muttered loud enough for her to hear, "We'll see."

# Chapter 4

## Ellison

After a quick shower, I sniffed Jack's shirt, drawing the scent of his laundry detergent deep into my lungs, before pulling it over my head. Stepping into his boxers, I couldn't help but think I needed to detour to his laundry room to see what brand he used, so I could be surrounded by the smell every day. Then again, I wouldn't be able to do my job because I'd be distracted by memories of the night we'd spent together. I guessed that plan was out the window. If only my job literally wasn't life or death, the tradeoff might be worth it. Jack smelled *that* good.

I stopped in the foyer to grab my cell phone, unaccustomed to going more than a couple hours without checking it. Even when I wasn't on call, it wasn't rare for me to get calls with questions about my patients. A quick glance confirmed I'd only missed one call from the hospital, but they hadn't left a message so it must not have been urgent. As I heaved a sigh of relief, my phone rang with an incoming call—not from the hospital, but from my date. The one I'd completely forgotten about and had apparently stood up this morning, since I was supposed to have met him five minutes ago.

"Ellison Reed," I answered out of habit.

"I'm running a little late. Traffic was backed up because of an accident," Richard grumbled.

Some of my guilt evaporated at the irritation evident in his tone. I'd seen the results of too many accidents first-hand to ever feel anything but relieved my car wasn't involved and hopeful nobody was injured whenever I drove past one. Plus, as hypocritical as it was of me, I was a little bothered that he had waited until he was already late before calling me. I knew it was ridiculous, considering I was standing in the middle of Jack's house, dressed in his clothes after spending the night in his bed, but I was annoyed nonetheless.

"I'm sorry, Richard, but something's come up and I won't be able to make it today."

"Or any day," Jack growled in my ear, sneaking up on me and grinding his hips against my ass to demonstrate exactly what had come up. Again.

I shook my head to clear my thoughts, turning in his arms to press my palm against his mouth so he couldn't interrupt my call. Cancelling a date after it was supposed to have already begun was bad enough, I refused to do it with Jack whispering in my ear. Or even worse, not bothering to keep his voice down and making it clear to Richard exactly why I wasn't going to keep our date.

"I can't say I'm not disappointed, but I guess that's what happens when you're dating a successful surgeon. Do you think you'll be able to drive up later today or even tomorrow morning?"

*Dating?* How had my accepting one date with this guy turned into us dating? I should have realized he was going to turn into a Grade-A Clinger based on how many times he'd asked me out. Persistence wasn't always a good thing in a man, sometimes it was a sign of what's to come if you said yes.

"No, I won't be able to make it today or tomorrow."

Jack's eyes flared, and I felt his lips move against my skin. If the way his body tensed was any indication, he wasn't happy with the direction of my conversation with Richard, who was still jabbering off dates in my ear.

"Next weekend isn't good for me, either."

Jack's arms crossed over his chest while he leveled me with a glare. His eyebrow was quirked up in a challenging manner. We'd been friends long enough for me to know I didn't want him to decide he needed to take control of this discussion, not unless I wanted to switch gyms. And I liked my gym, dammit.

"As much as I appreciate your offer to reschedule, I probably shouldn't have taken you up on your offer in the first place, Richard."

"C'mon, Ellison. Don't back out now. It took me forever to get you to say yes in the first place. I'd hate to have to ask you another dozen times to hear you say it again."

Maybe Jack was right, and Richard really was a loser who wanted to get into my pants. A very persistent loser who might force me to switch gyms anyway. Why had I agreed to this date in the first place?

*Oh, yeah.* I returned Jack's glare with one of my own. I'd been caught in a weak moment while trying to convince myself I should date someone else because Jack was just my friend. Really, an argument could easily be made that this whole situation was his fault for not making a move sooner.

I dropped my hand away from his mouth and muttered into the phone, "Asking me another dozen times isn't going to change anything. I'm not going to meet you today and I won't be saying yes to you in the future."

"That's what you told me the fifth time I asked you out."

He'd kept track of my responses? I made a mental note to check out other gyms in the very near future. Avoiding the creepy guy I'd almost spent the day with was now a top priority for me. And night, gag!

"It's not going to happen, Richard. Not the next time you ask, or a dozen times after that. So do us both a favor and stop asking me."

I disconnected the call while he was in the middle of arguing with me. I'd clearly had a close call with him and he wasn't worth any more of my time, not when I had the object of my own obsession standing right in front of me—grinning, the smug bastard.

"It's a good thing you made it clear you weren't interested. There's only room for one dick in this relationship and it sure as hell isn't him."

"I'll have you know, Richard doesn't like to be called Dick," I countered, while doing a little dance in my head over the fact that Jack had just called whatever was happening between us a relationship.

He tugged on my arm, leading me into the living room and pulling me down so I was straddling his lap on the couch. "How about you worry about this dick instead," he murmured in my ear, grinding his hips upwards.

His hot length bumped against my clit, making me shudder. I twined my arms around his neck and pushed my knees into the cushions on either side of his hips as I moved over him. His hands slid under my shirt, skimming up my back. I circled my hips and his fingers dug into my skin. Then his lips were on mine, his tongue pushing into my mouth and exploring. One of his hands slid upwards, fisting in my hair and angling my head as he deepened his kiss.

My pussy had been sore earlier, but now it was aching for a different reason. I rubbed against him with purpose, dry humping his cock until I felt my body tightening. Groaning, he pulled me closer, my tits pressed hard against his chest and his hardened length as close to my body as it could get with clothes between us. Pleasure started to pump through my body, only to be interrupted by the sound of my phone ringing. A-fucking-gain.

"No," I whimpered.

Jack released his hold on my hair, reaching out an arm to snag my phone from where I'd dropped it on the cushion next to us.

"She might have been nice about it, but I'm not going to bother because we both know there's only one way you're gonna back off from her and that's when you realize she's already taken. Stay away from what's mine."

I sucked in a breath at the possessiveness evident in his tone, my eyes dropping down to the screen when he swiped his thumb across it to disconnect the call. Only there was one problem. The number on the display wasn't Richard's. The area code wasn't even local. The call had come from Minneapolis. *Minneapolis!*

"No!" I cried out, grabbing the phone from his hand and jumping off his lap.

I paced away from him, pressing the number in my call history to call back.

"Dr. Reed?"

The male voice on the other end of the line sounded confused, understandably so, considering what Jack had told him.

"Yes, this is she. I'm sorry I missed your call just now."

"How odd," he muttered. "There must have been a switch up with the lines or something."

I wasn't about to admit to the true origins of the "or something" in this situation. "To whom am I speaking?"

"Oh, yes. I'm Declan McGowan, head of Pediatrics at Children's Minneapolis. I'm sorry to call you out of the blue like this, but we have an unexpected opening for our Chief of Pediatric Surgery and were hoping you'd consider taking the position. I know it's unorthodox, but considering our current Chief barely beat you out for the position, the board thought we could bypass some of the steps in the hiring process if you were still interested."

My heart pounded wildly in my chest. I'd been crushed when I'd lost the spot as their Chief of Surgery to another candidate last year. It wasn't that I was unhappy with my current job, but this was a big promotion at a well-respected hospital. I swiveled around, my eyes landing on Jack. Dream job, dream man. Different cities. Damn my luck.

# Chapter 5

## JACK

I couldn't hear the other side of the conversation but I watched closely as Ellison's expression went from surprised to ecstatic. Then she turned to look at me and it shifted once again, this time to indecision. Whatever the person on the line was saying was clearly confusing her and it pissed me off. We were happening. End of story.

I frowned, tempted to take her phone and play a permanent game of "Keep Away." Of course, the doctor in me would never separate her from her connection to the hospital. He would, however, hang up on the fucker making her question our relationship.

She turned away from me, her phone to her ear, and moved to leave the room. Not fucking happening. I snagged her arm and tugged her back into my lap. She scowled at me but gave up struggling to move when she realized I wasn't going to budge.

"Thank you for the opportunity, Declan."

*Declan?* What kind of a man was named Declan? A man with a pussy, that's who.

"I know you need an answer soon, however my"—she glanced at me—"situation has changed since we last spoke."

I was getting really irritated at being left out of this conversation. I made a grab for her phone so I could listen in but she batted my hand away and pinched the skin so hard I yelped in pain.

"Sorry, one of my patients was just given a shot. Anyway, could I have some time to think it over?"

I growled and ended up with her hand pressed over my mouth again. Think what over, dammit?

"Great. Thank you, Declan. I'll be in touch soon."

She pushed the disconnect button on the phone then smacked my shoulder. "You're such an asshole sometimes, Jack!"

"Who the fuck was that?" I demanded.

She sighed. "Let me have a little time to process, then we'll discuss it, I promise."

I was about to argue, but the feel of her lips on mine and her hot little pussy rubbing against my still hard cock distracted me. She placed little kisses along my jaw until she was by my ear. "Who owns my pussy, honey?"

"You better fucking know who you belong to, Ellie," I snarled as I cupped her ass and yanked her closer, leaving absolutely no room between us. I ripped my shirt from over her head and latched onto a nipple, squeezing her ass hard as I sucked. Removing one hand, I freed my dick from my boxers and shoved the overly large boxers to the side, baring her dripping pussy.

"You're so fucking wet for me, baby. Only for me, right? You're drenched for the man who owns this pussy?" She moaned and I grabbed her hips to slam her down onto my cock as I surged inside of her. One thrust and I was fully seated inside her, her tight, slick walls gripping me, sucking me impossibly deeper.

We both groaned and after the phone calls and her change in attitude after the last one, I had no control left. I drove up into her, bringing her down hard as I entered her over and over, rubbing against her clit every time. My lips licked, bit, and sucked on her large, diamond hard nipples. I loved the way they felt in my mouth, tasted on my tongue.

My hands journeyed from her hips to the firm, round globes of her ass, spreading the cheeks. The middle finger of my right hand ringed her puckered little hole and when she cried out in pleasure, I put the tip inside as I brought her down one last time and we shattered together.

I emptied inside her, long jets of come filling her as I silently cheered my boys on, encouraging them to reach the finish line. I quickly shifted so we were lying on the couch with her trapped below me, staying buried deep inside her. I didn't want any of that shit leaking out. She didn't seem to mind, sighing and wrapping her legs around my waist.

I didn't want to start our relationship off with secrets or dishonesty, so I decided it was time to have the condom conversation, right after I'd buttered her up (go ahead, laugh. I get it) and was still filling her with my cock.

I kissed her deeply first. "Baby, we need to talk," I mumbled against her lips.

"Hmmmm?" her tone was relaxed and mellow. I wasn't above taking advantage of her agreeable mood.

"You know we didn't use condoms last night? Or this morning?"

She groaned, "Shit. Damn you and your giant cock, Jack Halston. I can't think when you're fucking my brains out."

I didn't even try to hide my smug grin.

She rolled her eyes. "You need to figure out how to use a condom, Jack. I swear to all that is holy, if you got me pregnant with your baby, I'm going to kick your ass. Besides, I'd probably be forced to have a C-section because it will inevitably inherit your mammoth ego and a head that large won't fit out of my vagina."

"I'm a doctor, Ellie, I know how to use a fucking condom." I brought my face inches from hers, my expression turning serious. "I just chose not to because I'm going to knock you up, baby. I'm going to fuck you every chance I get until I'm sure my kid is growing in this sexy belly."

Ellison's jaw dropped in shock, and I nodded firmly to emphasize my determination to make this happen.

"And, let's get this out in the open so you can come to terms with it sooner rather than later. If your house isn't up for sale before you find out you're pregnant, you bet your ass I will handle that shit." I softened and kissed her sweetly, "I want you in my bed every night, Ellie. I want to wake up holding you in my arms. And I definitely want to have easy access to the pussy I own."

Her eyes had begun to melt at my words but the last sentence snapped her out of the haze. *Way to go, dipshit.*

She took a deep breath and stared at me, clearly trying to maintain a semblance of calm and control. I was still fully seated inside her and all this talk about babies and having her whenever I wanted had turned my semi-hard erection into stone. I shifted hoping to gain a little relief in another position.

At the movement inside her, Ellison glared at me and tried to push me off of her. Her efforts were futile. I outweighed her by at least a hundred pounds.

"You can't just decide to get me pregnant, Jack!" she exclaimed.

I sealed my mouth over hers before mumbling, "Sure I can," against her lips. Moving with slow, torturous strokes, I drove her out of her fucking mind until she exploded in my arms and I filled her with even more of my seed.

"See?" I murmured.

"I—I, um ... no, you, um," she stuttered, her mind seemingly in a confused and disconnected state.

I pulled out of her, my chest figuratively puffing up at her small sound of protest. Picking her up, she wrapped herself around me like she did when I carried her. I started for my room and the shower, but right when I set her on the counter, my cell phone started ringing.

"Fuck," I muttered. I swiftly stalked across the bedroom to grab it from the dresser. "Dr. Halston," I answered.

"Doctor," Debbie, the shift supervisor said urgently, "Heather developed a complication. The on call doctor wants to open her up again, but I knew you'd want to be the one."

"I'll be there in twenty minutes," I responded before hanging up and tossing my phone on the bed. I rushed into the bathroom and turned the shower on.

"I'm sorry, baby, I've got to go in."

Ellie frowned. "Heather?"

I nodded and hopped into the glass stall. She hurried in after me and began to rush through a shower too. I should have expected she would want to be there as well. Heather was also her patient.

Our personal stuff would have to wait. We reached the hospital and I confirmed Heather needed additional surgery. I wanted to put my fist through a wall, but my volatile reaction wouldn't help either of us. Ellison pulled me into the scrub room and helped me prep. Her presence soothed my turbulent emotions, infusing me with calm and determination.

# Chapter 6

## Ellison

Long hours and exhaustion were the norm in a surgeon's life, but they were hell on relationships. Even when both people were doctors apparently. Jack and I had spent so many hours at the hospital since Heather's emergency surgery that we hadn't been able to revisit the whole 'trying to knock me up' conversation. Not that it had stopped him from giving his pregnancy plan another go or two—or twelve. I'd taken to putting condoms in my purse, lab coat pockets, his pockets, both our cars... pretty much everywhere. Not that it had done a lick of good. In the heat of the moment, I never remembered to ask him to put one on, and he sure as hell never offered. I was beginning to wonder if it was my subconscious trying to tell me I actually wanted the smug bastard to knock me up.

The timing was horrible, though, with the offer of my dream job dropping in my lap. A decision I'd successfully avoided thinking about over the last week, too. Judging by the increasing frequency of the calls coming from Declan, time was running out. The ringing of my phone pulled me out of my thoughts. I glanced down and recognized the number on the display.

*Speak of the devil.*

"Hey, Declan," I answered. "I'm sorry I haven't been able to get back to you with a response yet."

"No apology needed, Ellison," he assured me. "I expect my call caught you unaware after we went with a different candidate initially."

"It definitely was unexpected," I confirmed.

"The board and I want to make it clear how committed we are to having you on our team."

He was telling me exactly what I would have given almost anything to hear a year ago. "I appreciate that, Declan, and you know how excited I was by the prospect of working for you when I interviewed last year."

"Why do I hear a but in there somewhere?"

"I'm just not sure I want to make the move right now," I sighed.

"Give me a chance to convince you otherwise. Let me take you to lunch so we can talk it through face-to-face."

"Lunch?" I repeated. How would that even work with him in Minneapolis and me in Rock Springs? "When?"

"Today."

His answer shocked me, stopping me in my tracks as I walked through the hospital corridor. "Are you in Nebraska?"

"I told you the board and I wanted to convince you of how serious we are about you taking this job."

"So you hopped on a plane to come to me? For lunch?" I sputtered, feeling flattered by the lengths to which they were willing to go to talk to me about the job. It helped soothe some of the sting from when they'd not selected me for it previously.

"I will if you tell me you're available for lunch today."

My stomach growled, reminding me I'd skipped breakfast. Turning down a free lunch was silly. "Sure, I can do lunch."

"Great! I'll pick you up at the hospital?"

"Sure," I drawled, thinking about how I could make sure we didn't run into Jack while he was here. Not only hadn't we talked about the condom situation, I still hadn't mentioned the job offer either.

"Mmmm," I murmured, savoring the flavor of my bacon wrapped filet. Declan had gone all out, picking me up in a town car and taking me to one of the best steakhouses in town. It was a good thing I didn't have a heavy case load this afternoon, because I could easily see a nap in the sleep room in my near future.

"Smart, successful, gorgeous, and you actually eat real food instead of weeds." Declan's tone was filled with masculine approval.

My eyes popped open in surprise. I'd been enjoying my food so much, I'd kind of forgotten he was there for a minute. I ducked my head in embarrassment and set my fork down on my almost empty plate. Skipping breakfast hadn't been a smart idea since I'd been hungry enough to devour my entire steak in a matter of minutes. "I definitely enjoyed my food," I mumbled.

Declan reached out to grab my hand and squeeze it. I slid my hand away and dropped it onto my lap. *Awkward.*

"I meant it as a compliment, Ellison."

"Thanks," I whispered.

"You done?"

"Yeah," I confirmed, fidgeting in my seat, suddenly aware of how we'd been seated together in a corner booth.

He waved the waiter over, and he cleared the table, leaving the check behind for Declan.

"I've already given you my pitch." And he had, both the last time I'd interviewed and during our lunch. "Not to sound conceited, but I know we have a lot to offer at Children's Minneapolis."

"You do," I replied, nodding in understanding.

"When we spoke last week, you mentioned your situation had changed." His gaze dropped to where my hands were folded in my lap before rising to meet mine again. "I can only assume it's your personal life since our research hadn't indicated anything different in your current position."

"It is." I kept my answer short because I didn't really want to get into it with him.

Declan cocked his head to the side, his gaze speculative as he scanned my face. "I hope you don't mind if I get a little personal with you for a moment."

I waved a hand in a circular motion, giving him permission to continue since I was curious where he was going to take this.

"I'd hate to see you pass up an opportunity like this because of a guy, especially when there will be opportunities for romance in Minneapolis for you."

"Erm..." I sputtered, completely flustered and unsure how to respond.

"Let me be blunt." *Like he wasn't already?* "I didn't see a ring on your finger, so I've got to think this guy probably isn't worth the sacrifice. Not when you can take the job with us and let me take you out on a date after you get settled in up there."

*Oh, for criminy's sake.* Was I putting off irresistible pheromones or something? First, Richard got all weird when I tried to let him down easily, and then here was Declan trying to lure me into the job in Minneapolis, using himself as bait. Not to mention, Jack doing his best to knock me up.

"That's incredibly kind of you to offer," I murmured, glancing down at my phone as it vibrated in my hand. "And as much as I'd love to discuss this further," —*not*— "they need me back at the hospital."

"They" was really Jack since he was the one trying to reach me. I sent him a quick text, letting him know I was on my way back and chuckled softly at the series of rapid-fire texts which followed.

**Jack:** I missed you for lunch. You took my favorite meal with you. I had a taste for honey.

**Jack:** Where did you go?

**Jack:** Wanna meet me in my office for a quickie?

**Jack:** I promise to do my best to make you scream, but I'll keep your mouth busy so nobody can hear you.

**Me**: Poor, starving boy. I'll be there in 5 minutes.

*Damn that man!* The ride back to the hospital couldn't go fast enough since it was already awkward, and that was before I was blushing wildly and my panties were damp from the images Jack had put in my head. I stayed super quiet, not wanting to do anything to make

Declan think the visible signs of arousal were due to him.

When the car pulled up in front of the hospital, I practically leapt from the vehicle. Unfortunately, Declan followed behind me and insisted on walking me back inside. And my bad luck turned worse as I caught sight of Jack through the glass doors. He didn't give us a chance to make it inside before he stormed through the doors to meet me on the sidewalk and stake his claim.

"Ellie," he growled, his mouth crashing down on mine in a kiss which screamed possessiveness. When he lifted his head, my knees were weak and I was holding on to his arms for dear life.

Declan cleared his throat, drawing my attention to him, right along with Jack's.

"Dr. Jack Halston," he announced, holding his hand out to shake Declan's. "Ellie's fiancé."

*Say what now?* Had I completely missed his proposal at some point this week?

Declan's gaze dropped to my ringless finger before he chuckled softly. "Dr. Declan McGowan from Children's Minneapolis. I was in town trying to tempt Ellison into joining our team. Considering how things went down last year, I figured a little bit of wooing was in order."

Jack's jaw twitched and he practically growled out his response. "Thanks for treating my girl to lunch, but I've got her from here." I shivered at the hint of sensual threat in his words. I had a feeling he was going to make me pay for not talking to him about the job offer soon.

## Chapter 7

## JACK

As a doctor, I understood the results of physical violence more than most, but this guy was going to find himself well acquainted with my fist if he didn't get the fuck out of there, fast.

I slipped my arm around Ellison and squeezed her waist, gluing her to my side. Declan (the pussy) was smiling like a cocky son of a bitch, and I glared while Ellison said goodbye and promised to call him. My fingers dug in a little harder, a reflex at the thought of her leaving me and conveying my irritation with her.

She extended her hand and I repressed the need to snatch it back, not wanting even the smallest touch of their skin. Declan finally turned to leave and I kept Ellison beside me as I walked back through the sliding glass doors into the hospital lobby.

"Hey, Dr. Halston, Dr. Reed," greeted a nurse in pink scrubs behind the registration desk. I jerked my chin in response and Ellison gave a weak wave with her free hand. Keeping steady on my path, I headed straight for my office, basically ignoring everyone on the way. Once we reached it, I guided her inside before turning and slamming the door shut. I took a second to calm myself, then turned to face her.

"Care to explain why you're keeping secrets from me and allowing other men to take you out?" I stalked over to her, forcing her to back up, but she only had a few inches before she was pinned between me and the desk. "And, let's be clear about one thing, there is no fucking way you are taking another job and moving away from me. You are mine, Ellison. Or haven't I made that quite obvious by keeping you in my bed every night and doing my damnedest to plant my kid in you?"

Ellison's eyes narrowed and she frowned at me before making an effort to push me away. She might as well be trying to move a block of stone. I wasn't going anywhere until she understood the situation.

"Listen, you big, overbearing caveman," she growled, "you don't make my decisions for me!"

I leaned in until our faces were a breath away. "I think we both know I don't need to. You know you're mine, baby." I grabbed hold of her ass and tugged her body flush against mine. "Or you wouldn't let my bare cock into your honeyed pussy." Lifting her up, I pressed the bulge in my pants into the cradle of her thighs. "Maybe you need a reminder," I rumbled before slamming my mouth down on hers.

"Dr. Reed," a disembodied voice called over the PA system. "You're needed in pediatrics." Fuck! I let her down, making sure she felt the slide of our bodies the whole way.

The page was repeated and I stepped back, giving her room to get around me and leave the office. She shook her head, evidently trying to clear away the thick haze of lust around us. She didn't make eye contact as she headed for the door, so I grabbed her arm forcing her to stop and turn back to me.

"I'll be continuing with my reminder later." Then I planted a quick kiss on her swollen lips and released her.

She pivoted and stepped over the threshold, muttering, "We'll see," and throwing my own words back at me. A grin stole over my face and I shook my head. I fucking loved that woman.

It turned out Ellison had to go into an emergency surgery and I had a scheduled case an hour after she was paged. However, I was still done before her and I hovered around her scrub room, lying in wait, ready to pounce. She finished up and I stayed out of sight until she'd washed and changed back into her street clothes and white lab coat.

I was lounging several feet down the hall and when she saw me, she hesitated for a moment, then lifted her chin stubbornly and continued toward me. It was fucking hot when she got riled and I was about to fan the flame. The thought had my already hard cock fighting like mad to be released and bury itself into her hot, wet pussy.

She began to walk past me without comment. It was adorable how she thought she'd get away with it. I placed a hand between her shoulder blades, the other twisting the knob on the nearest door. Firmly, I steered her through the opening. I shut the door and looked around, realizing we were in a storage closet. I mentally shrugged. It would do.

Ellison was glowering at me, her arms folded across her chest, lifting her breasts, and a hip cocked out.

"Can I help you, Dr. Halston?" she gritted through her teeth. Backing her into the wall, I pressed against her.

"You can scream, Dr. Halston, when I make you come so hard you see fucking stars."

She tried to stifle it, but I heard her little gasp and glanced down to see her nipples hardened into mouthwatering peaks.

"I think you need a cold shower and a craniotomy to remove some of your ego and the Neanderthal inside you," she said with a dismissive air, trying and failing to hide how turned on she was.

"You know you love my cocky caveman." I grinned with smug confidence. "And his big cock."

Before she could protest any further, I gave in to my desperation to claim her, taking her lips in an aggressive kiss. I wanted to overwhelm *her*, but in all reality, love, need, and passion crashed over *me*, too.

Her blouse had buttons down the front and it was easily ripped open, the buttons flying out and pinging off of the shelves. I shoved down the cups of her sexy, pink, lace bra. Her tits spilled out, but were held up by the underwire. It was as though they were being offered up to me, and I took full advantage, sucking on them like they were my favorite candy. They weren't far off anyway.

Ellison moaned, thrusting her tits forward, her hands going to my hair, gripping it to keep me close. Yeah, there was no need, I wasn't going fucking anywhere until I'd accomplished my goal. My mouth still lavishing her tits with attention, I palmed her ass and lifted her so her legs immediately circled my waist. The feeling of her thighs clamping hard almost made me spill right then, but I held back, not wanting to come until I was deep inside her and my boys had a chance to swim their little asses right to her eggs. If I hadn't done so already, this time, I was going to get her good and pregnant.

I dropped her to the ground and flipped positions so I was the one leaning on the wall. My mouth returned to hers and I used my foot to feel around, until it hit something hard. Tearing my mouth away, my hands twisted and plucked at her nipples, while I looked to see and found a large, empty crate on my left. I let Ellison go for a minute to grab a stack of towels and drop them onto the top of the crate. I lowered my zipper and freed my cock. It was so hard, I hissed in pain when the fabric caught. Turning her around, I cupped her tits, massaging them before dragging my hands down to lift the hem of her skirt (thank fuck she wore one that day) and tuck it into her waistband. Then I returned one palm to a big, round tit, the other sliding through her wetness.

"I love how wet you get for me, baby. Fucking drenched."

"Oh, Jack," she moaned.

I carefully descended down to the top of the crate, both arms curling around so they were each on an inner thigh. My legs extended between her legs and I put pressure on them to widen her stance. When she was right where I wanted her, I was staring at the most perfect ass I'd ever seen and eyed the tiny string holding her thong together. It was easy to snap before I used a gentle palm on her back to bend her slightly forward, baring her pink, pussy to me. Her clit was swollen and begging, so I appeased it by sucking it into my mouth.

"Oh, fuck!" Ellie screamed. I knew I should cover her mouth or do something to keep her quiet, but it was the least of my worries. And, I got off on her loud exclamations of pleasure. Licking from top to bottom, I added a finger to mimic what my cock was going to be doing to her soon.

"Mmmmm. I need a honey snack," I purred. "My snack only, right, Ellie?" I asked with a little more force. When she didn't answer right away, I pinched her clit while my tongue plunged inside her.

"Yes!" she cried out.

"Good girl. Who owns this pussy, baby?"

"You," she panted. I wanted to ask her if she loved me but I chickened out and brought her to a screaming orgasm instead.

Gripping her hips, I widened my own legs to keep her open as I guided her down enough to line my cock up and then slammed her down onto it. We both gasped at the feel of being joined together so intimately. With her position keeping her wide, I bent my knees and they came up enough so she could lean forward and rest against them. It bared her spectacular ass again and the flesh begged to be spanked. A sharp crack rang through the sound of our panting and otherwise quiet closet.

Ellie jerked and it seated me even deeper.

"Oh, fuck yes, baby!" I cried out.

I wrapped my fingers around the edges of the crate, and used the pressure of my feet on the floor for leverage, and began to thrust up hard enough to bounce her body and make it slam back down each time. Ellie sat up straight and squeezed the fuck out of my dick every time she landed.

"Yes, yes, yes," she chanted, adding a "harder, Jack!" in there for good measure.

I put every bit of my strength into fucking her. When I felt the telling clenching of her walls, I kept a tight grip on her body, her back tight against my front, and pushed to my feet. Turning, I growled, "Grab the shelf, baby. Don't let go."

Once her hands were secure, I wrapped her legs backwards around my hips, then drove into her, gaining speed every time she cried out until I was fucking her with frenzy. I had no rhythm, no finesse, it was raw, animalistic fucking.

She screamed my name as her body shuddered, her pussy strangling my cock, sucking it in as I thrust three more times before exploding. I pushed against her and with her legs so high up, I was in a good position to seal our groins together, holding myself inside so it would be as deep as possible as I shot my load and kept any from leaking out.

Finally, we both lost the strength to hold our position and I slipped out of her, letting her feet down as I did. She mewled in protest and mentally, my chest swelled with pride at satisfying my woman. I held her against me, leaning my head so my mouth was at her ear.

"Was that a sufficient reminder, Ellie?" My hands slid down her soft skin to splay over her belly. "This time, I know I gave you my baby. You are mine Ellie, you and our babies."

Ellie jerked at my words. "Babies? As in, plural?"

I nuzzled her neck, "At least four. I want lots of little Ellies running around.

"*At least* four?" she exclaimed. "When the fuck am I going to have time to raise four kids and be a doctor?"

I kissed her ear. "I have no doubt you could handle it baby. You're the strongest woman I've ever met." Even though the words were one hundred percent true, I smiled in triumph as I felt her melt a little. "And, I'll be there to help you every step of the way."

She snorted and I turned her around to face me, frowning and hurt. "You don't believe I'll be a good dad?"

She looked chagrined. "No, Jack. I'm sorry. I think you'll be an amazing dad, but four kids with two doctors for parents? I can't help wondering if you're banking on me wanting to quit and stay home with our kids."

I scowled, but realized how easy it would be for her to come to this conclusion and softened my expression. "I never considered taking away your career, Ellie. It's part of you just like it is me. You're an amazing doctor. I hope you trust me enough to believe me."

She gave me a small smile, but I could tell she wasn't entirely convinced. The only thing I could do was prove it. I had the rest of our lives to do it, so I pushed it away for another day.

# Chapter 8

## Ellison

"We need to stop over at Wyatt and Bailey's house on our way home."

My eyebrows practically climbed all the way up to my hairline at the casual way Jack tossed his comment out, as though it wasn't a big deal. Today had already been interesting with Jack's reaction to my lunch with Declan. Meeting part of his family would just cap the day off, especially since I'd been looking forward to changing out of my work clothes and pouring myself a big glass of wine. Annoyed, I grumbled under my breath, "I know you've been working all day and you're stuck in scrubs instead of the kickass outfit you put on this morning because I ruined your blouse when I ripped it from your body, but I'm sure my family will love you anyway." I mimicked what I wished he would have said.

"I promise it won't take long, and you look hot as fuck in those scrubs, just like you do in anything you wear." Apparently, I hadn't been quiet enough. *Whoopsie.* "My nephew, Jack, has been running a fever all day and my sister wants me to stop by to make sure it's nothing serious."

*Oh, no!* I felt guilty for being such a grump. "Of course we should go."

"He usually eats like a little pig, but Bailey said he's barely eating and incredibly irritable. Plus, he's been rubbing his ear a lot today. It's probably nothing more than teething his first tooth, but she wants to rule out other possible causes like an ear infection and couldn't get them in to see the twins' pediatrician until tomorrow afternoon."

"Poor baby," I sighed, turning towards him and offering a commiserating smile. "But it's nice that Uncle Jack can race to the rescue."

He reached over and gave my thigh a quick squeeze as he pulled into the driveway. "If it's nice for Jack and Julia to have a surgeon for their uncle, imagine how lucky our kids will be to have two surgeons for their mom and dad."

*Our kids.* How was it possible we were both calling them that already? My hand drifted down to my stomach, and I tried to imagine what it would be like if I were pregnant with his baby. Neither of us had used the L-word yet and I'd been offered my dream job in another state. The timing wouldn't be good for a baby, at all.

And then we walked into his sister's house, and my biological clock roared to life. I'd always thought Jack was handsome, but seeing him with his baby niece and nephew made him even more irresistible. There really wasn't anything like a sexy man with a baby in his arms to make your ovaries feel like they were about to explode. Sneaky bastard, if baby Jack hadn't been sick, I would have been positive he'd planned our visit for precisely this reason.

"I'm so happy to finally meet you," Bailey whispered to me as we both watched from the doorway while Jack checked his namesake over. Or I looked on while she stared at me appraisingly until I felt a blush creep up my cheeks.

"Finally? Jack and I haven't been a couple very long."

She chuckled softly. "Maybe not, but I've been hearing your name pop up in conversation with my brother more and more over the last six months."

I tore my attention away from the sight of Jack with a look of pure adoration on his face as he stared down at the adorable baby boy in his arms, one long finger rubbing along his gums. It wasn't easy, but I was intrigued by what Bailey had just said. "Really?" She nodded, and I lowered my voice before continuing the conversation. "When did Jack first mention me?"

Bailey cocked her head to the side and tapped her bottom lip with a finger. "It's been at least a year because I feel like I was pregnant enough to just be in maternity clothes and the babies are seven months old."

"Huh," I murmured, my gaze flitting back to Jack. "I'm surprised it was that long ago. We didn't know each other very well back then."

"It wasn't what he said but how he said it," she explained. "You were working a case together and his eyes lit up when he mentioned your role in helping to save the patient. The way he looked when he said your name, combined with how complimentary he was about your surgical skills put you on my sisterly radar."

"He's not exactly known around the hospital for offering praise to other doctors."

Bailey's soft chuckle turned into a belly laugh, drawing Jack's gaze our way. "This doesn't surprise me. I love my brother dearly, but he can be a bit arrogant. Remind me to tell you the story of how he reacted to Wyatt's and my relationship some time."

Jack glared at his sister before looking back down at the baby in his arms. "Your mommy is being a brat, buddy. But it's a good thing, because she reminded me that you and I need to have a talk about what it means to be a big brother." He stood up and walked over to the crib decorated in pink where Julia slept peacefully.

"See your sister down there?" He leaned over so he and the baby could look at Julia. "Your toughest responsibility as her big brother is going to be to protect her from all the boys out there. You'll have a lot of help from your daddy and me, but there will be times when you're the only line of defense. Doesn't matter if the boy is your friend or not, a good guy or a bad one—you'll know he isn't good enough for Julia. None of them will be."

"Oh, for goodness sakes, Jack," Bailey huffed as she walked over to take her son from his arms. "He's too young to understand a single word you're saying."

"Hey, you can't blame me for giving him a head start." He threw his arms up defensively. "I just want to make up for the late one I got."

The look that passed between brother and sister brought tears to my eyes—Bailey's too.

She settled baby Jack into his crib before moving back to give her brother a hug. "You better not make me cry or Wyatt will try to kick your ass," she mumbled into his shirt.

"Nah," Jack answered. "He'll forgive me when I tell him his baby boy is about to get his first tooth and doesn't need to see the doctor tomorrow."

"What a relief," Bailey sighed, leaning back and beaming up at him.

"Besides, it's not like he could kick my ass anyway," Jack drawled, dropping a kiss on her head. "And we won't be here when he gets home."

He crossed the room, pulling me to his side and whispering in my ear. "We need to get home so I can make sure my reminder from this afternoon stuck, and give my swimmers another chance in case they didn't do their job earlier."

Jack didn't get any arguments from me. If I'd been wearing panties under my scrub pants, they would have been drenched.

Life with Jack moved lightning fast. One week we're work colleagues who flirt and the next we're friends who are practically joined at the hip. In one night, we moved from being firmly in the friend zone to an exclusive relationship. Then, I felt my biological clock ticking and the next week my period was late. It always came every twenty-eight days, like clockwork, and should have started two days ago. There was no sign of it starting anytime soon. I was pretty sure Jack had gotten his wish and knocked me up, which is how I found myself hiding in his bathroom first thing this morning while he was making breakfast. I'd peed on the stick three minutes ago and was trying to get up the nerves to look at the results.

"You can do this," I murmured softly. "No matter what the test says, you're a strong woman and you'll figure out the right thing to do."

My little pep talk wasn't doing anything to stop the flutter of butterflies in my belly. Taking a deep breath, I picked up the stick from the bathroom counter and flipped it over.

*Not pregnant.*

The air left my lungs with a heaving sigh. The emotion I should have felt was relief since I wasn't sure I was ready for babies, let alone to have them with Jack. Although I'd known him through work for two years, we'd only really been a couple for two weeks. Plus, I still needed to decide what to do about the job offer from Children's Minneapolis. My brain knew this was probably for the best, but it seemed my heart had a different perspective because I felt like it was breaking.

Logic didn't factor into what I was feeling. I'd spent the last two days thinking maybe he'd been right and he'd gotten me pregnant. *How was I going to tell him I wasn't?* He didn't even know my period was late because I hadn't been ready to talk to him about the real possibility of me being pregnant. It seemed like the right decision at the time, but I wished I'd said something because then I wouldn't be facing this alone. Sitting on the side of the tub, sobbing into my hands, I came to a few realizations.

I loved Jack Halston.

I couldn't take the job in Minneapolis.

And I wanted to have his babies, all four of them.

My tears shifted into a chuckle snort at the irony. Back in my undergrad years, I'd been a little judgy towards the girls who were there for their "Mrs. Degree," but I was going to turn down a promotion because of a man. Not just any man, though. I had a feeling my fellow nerd girls would make the same decision if given a chance with Dr. Jack Halston. Too bad for them he was all mine.

# Chapter 9

## JACK

I placed a bowl of strawberries on a tray along with pancakes, syrup, and orange juice. I wanted to make sure my woman had a good breakfast because I had plans to wear her the fuck out today. It was rare for us to have a day where we were both off and I intended to spend it in bed.

Lifting the tray, I carefully walked to the bedroom and was surprised to see the bed empty. There was light coming from the bathroom door, so I set the tray on the dresser and padded over to the closed door. I turned the knob, and as it opened, I heard soft crying. Alarmed, I raced the rest of the way inside to see Ellison sitting on the edge of the tub, her elbows on her knees, her face buried in her hands.

I scooped her up and took her seat, settling her on my lap, tucking her head under my chin, then rubbing her back in slow circles.

"What's wrong, baby?"

She sniffled for another minute before lifting her head, her brown eyes watery with tears.

"I didn't think I wanted it," she whispered as more tears tracked down her cheeks.

I gently wiped them away with my thumb. "Wanted what?"

"The life you were planning for us, the one with four kids, two surgeons, one house, and a partridge in a pear tree."

Her words sounded wistful and I took it as a good sign. "Baby, I'd really prefer a dog, but if this is your way of telling me you're pregnant, we can have whatever fucking pets you want."

She began to cry in earnest, burying her face into my chest. I started to panic and wonder if I'd gotten it wrong. If she was trying to tell me she had decided to take the job in Minneapolis, I'd chain her to my bed until I convinced her she didn't belong anywhere but here with me. I knew her, though. No matter the amount of time we'd been together, she was a part of me and I had no doubt that we wanted the same future. It was up to me to make her see it.

My eyes suddenly caught sight of a white, plastic stick sitting on the counter.

Still holding Ellie close, I reached out one long arm and picked up the pregnancy test. I stared at it from the back for a moment, a little nervous. Are you sure you aren't the one with the vagina, dude?

Holding my breath, I flipped it over and the air came whooshing out in a rush.

Not Pregnant.

Chained to the bed it is.

I stood with her cradled in my arms and tossed the test into the garbage. Taking her to the bed, I lay her down and covered her body with mine.

"I told you before, Ellie. You're mine. I won't let you leave me. If you want to wait to start a family, I'll give you whatever you ask, except let you go. I love you and I know you love me. We were meant to be together and I'm going to keep you right here until I've convinced you it's true."

Her chocolate brown eyes widened as she stared into my face. "You—you love me?" she stuttered.

It dawned on me that I've laid myself bare to her, opened up my chest and gave her the ammunition to rip my heart out. Not for one second did I regret it, though. She was worth it. She was everything.

I brushed my lips over hers then leaned back to gaze at her beautiful face. "Yeah, Ellie. I love you. I'm sure I've loved you since the moment I first met you. It took me a while to realize you were everything I never knew I always wanted. Once I understood my feelings, I decided there was no other recourse but to make you mine. I know you love me, Ellie." I took a shuddering breath and made the last step into complete vulnerability. "Right?"

She glided her hands up my chest and neck until she was cupping my face. "I love you more than anything in this world, Jack. You're right, you own me. And, I don't want to wait. I want to have a family with you, now."

The relief I felt was overwhelmingly acute. Obviously I'd been more nervous than I'd thought. I grinned at her and melded our mouths together, pouring all of my love into the kiss.

I pulled back and stared at the gorgeous woman beneath me and noticed the dried tears on her face. After another quick kiss, I caressed her cheek, tracing the salty tracks. "No need to cry, baby. I'll fuck you as many times as I need to until you're swollen with my baby in your belly," I promised and was rewarded with the sweet sound of her laughter.

A thought crashed into me and I jumped from the bed and started for the door, halting after a few steps and whirling around. I pointed at her. "You. Stay."

She scrunched her cute little nose in distaste. "You better be practicing for when we have a dog, Dr. Halston."

I groaned helplessly. Whenever she called me Dr. Halston, it turned me the fuck on. I pointed to her once again and raced from the room, determined to get back as fast as possible. I practically flew down the back set of stairs to my office and snatched a small blue box from the drawer of my desk. Just as swiftly, I returned to our room and climbed back over her.

Satisfied she'd stayed where I put her, I kissed her forehead. "Good girl." She glared at me.

I put the most innocent expression on my face that I could manage. "I guess you don't want your treat for being obedient then?" I held up the petite box and her jaw dropped, an excited sparkle in her eye. "Did you think I was fucking around when I told the pussy I was your fiancé?" I grinned, remembering how I'd staked my fucking claim on my woman.

"You never said anything, I assumed—"

I cut her off, "Well, you were wrong. I was trying to think of a romantic way to propose, something incredibly romantic. But, I can't wait any longer. I need everyone to know you're not available. I own you."

She rolled her eyes, but there was a smile playing around the corners of her mouth. I untied the silky, white bow and removed the lid. Taking out a black, velvet box, I flipped it open to reveal a five-carat, cushion cut diamond, set in a diamond encrusted, platinum band. Ellie gasped, her face filled with awe as she touched the ring with the tips of her fingers, tracing it in the velvet display.

"It's stunning, Jack. I love it."

"You love who?" I asked gruffly, jealous of a stupid ring.

She winked at me. "I love you." Then I heard her mutter under her breath, "Almost as much."

"You're going to pay for that, baby," I grumbled. Taking the ring from the box, I slid it onto her trembling finger. "You know what this mean, right?" I asked warily, and then it occurred to me we hadn't discussed her ridiculous job offer. "No moving, no new job, no Declan," I spat his name, still fighting the urge to rearrange his face for trying to steal my girl.

Ellison huffed, "Do you have to steamroll everything?"

I frowned, offended at her accusation and a tad unsure what she meant. "No," I said with conviction. "But when my fiancée is considering moving out of state and"—I glared fiercely at her—"lets other men take her to lunch, I'm sure as fuck going to steamroll anything or anyone who gets in my way."

Her lips turned down into a pout, adorable and utterly irresistible. I drank from her lips until she bit my lip a little harder than usual.

"Fuck! What the hell, Ellie?"

"You distracted me."

"And?" I asked with a single raised eyebrow.

She scowled and it grew when I couldn't keep myself from grinning. I fucking loved her to pieces.

"I was going to tell you I'd decided not to take the job. I want to stay here, to be with you. But your damn caveman tactics stole my thunder. I wanted to tell you I was devastated not to be pregnant. I love you, Neanderthal and all."

I winked at her and smiled. "I'll make it up to you," I vowed before kissing her until she was breathless and quaking with need.

There was only one thing left to do before I could spend the rest of the day making her scream my name. Tearing my mouth from hers (no easy feat, I might add), I stretched over to grab her cell phone off of the nightstand.

"Call him, now," I demanded, handing her the phone.

She was watching me with amusement. "Call who?"

"Don't mess with me, baby. You've already guaranteed I'm going to punish you by making you orgasm as hard and as often as possible until you pass out. If you want to keep it up, you'll earn a round two."

She winked. "Promise?"

I laughed, but grabbed the phone away from her and looked for his contact info, pressing send before putting it on speaker. She made a grab for it, but I caught her wrists and held them locked in one hand above her head.

"Ellie!" Douche bag's voice came over the line and my hand tightened at the use of her nickname. My nickname. I opened my mouth to tell him off, but Ellison started talking.

"Declan," she replied.

"I hope you're calling to accept the job, and give me a chance."

This guy was pissing me off more and more. I could feel the flush of anger and knew my face had to be turning red.

"Um," Ellie was giving me a warning in her eyes, telling me to back off and let her handle it. I nodded jerkily, willing to acquiesce to her request, for the moment.

"No, I am incredibly flattered and it's certainly a very tempting offer." I growled at the idea she might find it tempting to leave me.

She hissed at me to shut up, quiet enough so it wouldn't carry into the phone.

"Please, Ellie. Give us a chanc—"

I'd had it. "Her name is Dr. Reed or soon to be Dr. Halston, whichever of those you prefer to call her," I snapped. "Actually, you won't be calling her anything. So back the fuck off and leave my woman alone."

I hit the disconnect button and dropped the phone onto the plush, carpeted floor. I didn't give her an opportunity to lash out at me. I busied myself with giving her six screaming orgasms until she passed out.

If possible, I was even more determined to knock my woman up. Alright boys, we're going to war.

# Chapter 10

## Ellison

Jack had been doing his best to turn that negative pregnancy test positive over the last few days, waking me up at least once every night to give it an extra try. He'd turned me into a walking zombie with all his attempts. I hadn't been this tired since my residency years. I used to be able to go for several days on very little sleep, but it looked like hitting my thirties meant I was too old to pull all-nighters anymore, even for sex.

I buried my face in my pillow when I felt the slide of the sheet on the bare skin of my back. "Must sleep."

My words were muffled but apparently clear enough for Jack to understand based on his deep chuckle. "Up and at 'em, baby. You've got things to do before I leave for my shift at the hospital."

"No," I moaned. "I really don't have anything I need to do."

"Are you sure about that?"

"Yeah," I confirmed. "I'm pretty sure we did all the things already last night. And super early this morning. As much as I love you and as hot as you are, I don't think I can handle any more orgasms until I get some sleep."

"I'm not talking about sex, Ellie."

*He wasn't?* That was certainly a surprise. I raised up on an elbow to look at him and practically fell over at the sight of what he was holding in his hand. "You know you're crazy, right?"

He waived the little white stick in my face. "You love my brand of crazy."

"I just took one three days ago, and it was negative," I grumbled, slumping back down on the mattress.

He shrugged his shoulders. "Maybe you peed on it wrong."

"I did no such thing!" I huffed. "I'm a board certified pediatric surgeon. Peeing on a stick isn't past my skill set."

"And yet your period is almost a week late, you're exhausted, and you shoved me off the bed last night when I tried to play with your tits," he quipped. "Something which would usually make you cream your panties."

"But the test was negative," I repeated.

He gripped my hands and tugged me from the bed, nudging me towards the bathroom. "As you so kindly pointed out already, you're a board certified surgeon. You should be familiar with the notion of false negatives."

"Do you really think that's what it was?" I whispered as I crossed through the doorway. As odd as it sounded, the possibility hadn't even crossed my mind. I'd been too upset to consider it.

"Only one way to find out," he replied.

I hiked up his shirt, the one I'd tugged on when he'd finally let me fall back asleep last night, and squatted down to sit on the toilet. "Out!" I ordered him.

"C'mon," he groused. "I want to be here every step of the way with you. We're in this together."

"The only way you're going to be in the bathroom during the peeing on the stick step is if the day ever comes when you're the one doing the peeing."

"Fine," he huffed before stepping out and closing the door behind him. He didn't give me long, though. As soon as I'd finished peeing and flushed, the door swung open again. He gave me just enough time to wash my hands, while he was busy wrapping the test in a washcloth, before he picked me up and carried me back to bed. Laying me gently down on the mattress, he quickly followed and looked at me with boyish delight in his eyes. "Is it time yet?"

"Not yet," I giggled. "You have to wait a couple more minutes."

"I guess I'd better find a way to pass the time," he murmured against my mouth, claiming them in a quick but deep kiss before trailing his lips lower. Along my jaw, down my neck, teasing the sides of my tits. He made it to my belly before he spoke again, whispering softly, "I think it's time to prove to your mommy that you're in there."

My breath caught in my throat at the sight of his dark head against my pale skin. "Please, please, please," I chanted as he reached for the washcloth and carefully lifted a corner to peek inside. The blinding smile which spread across his face gave me my answer before he could show me the test. It was positive. It had to be. I leaned over, bumping his shoulder to make room for me, and looked down at the digital screen.

*Pregnant.*

"We're pregnant."

"Damn straight you are," he confirmed, tossing the stick and washcloth to the floor and diving on top of me. "And now we need to celebrate."

If I'd been wearing them, my panties would have melted at his happiness. "How exactly do you plan to celebrate this news when you need to be at the hospital soon?"

His smile turned into a sly grin. "I've got an hour."

My head swiveled so I could peer at the clock on the bedside table. "No, you don't. You need to leave in like ten minutes."

"I set the clock ahead before I woke you up," he informed me, tugging my shirt over my head. "I wanted to make sure we had enough time to celebrate before I had to go."

"You were that confident?"

He tore his shirt off and shoved his boxers down his legs. "There wasn't a doubt in my mind, Ellie."

"How about you show me how you planned to spend that hour?"

He dropped a quick kiss to my belly and then settled in between my legs. "You're so fucking beautiful, baby," he murmured against the sensitive skin of my inner thigh. His breath was hot against my naked flesh as his tongue flicked out for a quick lick. "And I'm addicted to the taste of your honey."

That's all it took for me to suddenly be on the edge of a climax. He'd barely touched me, but that didn't stop my walls from clenching against his tongue when he slid it inside my pussy. His finger circled my clit, and I felt myself lose control. He moaned against my pussy, and vibrations were enough to send me flying over the edge. My legs shook as they tightened around his head while I came.

"I'll never grow tired of hearing your cries while I eat your pussy," he growled before he levered up onto his knees and pulled my hips until I shifted lower on the bed. Then he impaled me with one hard thrust. "But there's nothing better than the feeling of your wet pussy wrapped tightly around my cock, knowing my baby is growing inside your belly."

He began moving hard and fast, going deep with each powerful thrust but holding my hips gently all the while. Over and over again, with his eyes locked on mine the whole time. Sex with Jack had always been amazing, from the very first time, but this time was different. Better.

More. His ring was on my finger, and I was pregnant with his baby. His eyes were filled with lust, but it was tempered by love. So much love.

His strokes triggered a tingling in my spine, making my toes clench against the sheets. Then it hit me, a climax bigger than I'd ever felt before, making me scream his name until my voice was hoarse. He kept going, hammering into me until I'd come again and my legs felt like jelly. When I didn't think I could take any more, he planted himself deep one more time and groaned. His cock jerked, and the heat from his semen sparked another orgasm for me.

"You were made for me," he murmured as he pulled me tight. "I should have admitted it to myself two years ago. If I had, then you'd be pregnant with our second or third child by now."

Resting my head against his chest, I laughed softly. "It's hard to know what would have happened if either of us had made a move back then, but I love that we had two years to get to know each other the way we did."

"You're happy about the baby, then?" he asked, a hint of vulnerability in his tone.

"I'm so happy." Three little words but they held a depth of meaning, intended to clear away the doubt I'd instilled within this amazing man who loved me.

"Happy enough to marry me tomorrow?"

I laughed, thinking he was joking until I caught the look of utter seriousness on his face. I had no doubt he'd find a way for us to exchange our vows tomorrow if I agreed, but I didn't hesitate to give him my answer. "Yes, honey."

# Epilogue

## JACK

I gently placed my infant son in his crib, running a hand through his soft, feathery hair. Eric was a quiet baby and was already sleeping through the night. Turning on the monitor, I went into the hall and pulled the door so it was almost shut. I'd already tucked in my sweet little two-year-old, Addy, so I padded down the hall to the den where my beautiful wife was stretched out on the couch, watching a movie. Making a beeline for her, I lowered myself down so my body covered hers.

"I do believe both of our kids are asleep, Dr. Halston," I whispered as I began to nibble on her ear. "Whatever will we do with this time alone?"

Ellie tilted her head back, giving me more access to her neck, and I placed hot, wet, open-mouthed kisses down to the valley between her tits. She was wearing a loose tank and the neckline gaped so I hooked a finger in the fabric and tugged it down. I groaned at the sight of her naked tits, fuller from two kids and nursing our son. I licked around one before taking it into my mouth.

I bit the tip lightly and she gasped, every muscle in her body freezing, before she started shaking. I lifted my head, surprised she'd come so fast. However, her face wasn't lost in ecstasy. Nope, she was laughing, her mouth pinched as she tried to keep quiet.

"If I wasn't so secure in my ability to make you come, this could be a pretty big blow to my ego, baby."

She snickered and pointed behind me. "What were you saying about the kids being asleep?"

I levered myself up onto my elbows and twisted to look back.

A pillow was floating through the door, or at least, it looked as though it was. Really, it had two little feet, just barely visible underneath the large pillow. Small, delicate fingers grasped the edges and it was moving slowly, hesitantly.

I smiled in exasperated amusement. Addy had reached the stage where she was like an ostrich sticking their head in the sand. She seemed to believe if she couldn't see us, we couldn't see her.

"Addy," I said sternly. The pillow jerked and lowered, revealing her big brown eyes. They were open wide, shocked at having been discovered. It was adorable as fuck. My kids were the cutest, I didn't care what Wyatt said. I loved my nieces and nephews, but come on, my daughter was a fucking knockout.

"Back to bed, sneaky."

Her wide chocolate eyes filled with tears and I looked at Ellie frantically. She raised a brow and stared at me challengingly. *Shit.* I forgot about our bet. Ellie was convinced I couldn't hold firm with my baby girl when she cried. It was ridiculous. I was man enough to deal with her tears without caving.

I narrowed my eyes and glared at her, my heart starting to crack with the little sniffles coming from behind me. I took a deep breath and steeled myself against the overwhelming desire to scoop her up and give her anything and everything she wanted.

Pulling up Ellie's shirt, I climbed off of her and faced my Addy, crumbling at the sight of the big, fat tears rolling down her face. I swiftly moved to her and scooped her up in my embrace. Her small arms wound around my neck and she rested her head against my chest, her head tucked under my chin.

"Monsters, Daddy," she hiccupped. "I want to seep wif you and Mommy." My resolve was fast disappearing, then she played the trump card. "I'm scared." It was my job to protect my baby girl, to scare away the monsters, to be her hero, damn it.

"Sure, baby girl."

Ellie cleared her throat noisily and I glanced back to see her shaking her head. I threw her a pleading look but she had no sympathy, snickering at me again. *Callous, unfeeling woman!*

She finally stood and walked over to us. "You should sleep in your big girl bed, Addy. Daddy will check for monsters, then you go to sleep, okay?" She rubbed Addy's back in slow circles as she spoke.

Addy leaned back and looked up at me with soft, sad eyes. "Pwease, Daddy?" *Well, fuck.*

Ellie could obviously see I was about to give in and she shrugged before turning and muttering under her breath as she passed me. "Sucker."

I couldn't hide behind the pillow anymore. She was right, I was a complete sucker for my kids.

"I guess I'll have to wear something else to bed since ours will be so crowded," she called after she disappeared around the corner.

I quickly followed after her. "Something else?"

She glanced back with a smug smile. "Well, not so much something else as plain old something instead of nothing at all."

I hurried down the hall and into my daughter's bedroom, Ellie's laughter trailing behind me. Holding Addy, we checked the closet, under the bed, and every nook and crevice for monsters.

"See, baby girl? Nothing to be afraid of," I crooned, kissing her forehead. I bent to lay her in her new toddler, princess bed, but she clung tightly to me.

"Stay, Daddy?" she begged, tugging at my heartstrings. However, it had been a week since Ellie and I had an early night like this, one where we both weren't too tired for more than a quick fuck. I was dying to make love to my wife, to worship every inch of her delectable body, to taste her honey.

"Can you be my best girl, Addy? Show me how brave you are?" Her eyes teared up again and I swore a violent streak of curses for the shit I was going to take from Ellie for what I was about to do. Not to mention the shit from Bailey, Wyatt, and my dad, because Ellie would be on the phone first thing when she found out. My dick didn't give a fuck, so I gave up trying. "If you go right to sleep and be brave, you can have some of your birthday cake for breakfast."

Her eyes got wide, suddenly dry with no evidence of tears, and a smile spread over her sweet face as she nodded vigorously.

"Okay," I said as I tucked her in. "The faster you go to sleep, the faster morning will be here and you can have cake."

She immediately scrunched her eyes shut and snuggled into the teddy bear I placed in her arms. When she was settled, I raced to my bedroom, halting in disappointment when my wife wasn't waiting naked in bed for me.

Then I noticed the trail of clothes on the floor leading to the bathroom. When I opened the door, I stopped to admire the view of Ellie standing in the shower under the hot spray of water, cascading down her incredible body.

I shed my clothes at lightning speed and stepped in behind her, pulling her back against me and cupping her full tits. I fucking loved her body and it only got more luscious and beautiful with every baby.

"You promised her cake, didn't you?" she asked.

I ignored her and slipped a hand down to play with her pussy, making her moan. I was so fucking hard, I was afraid it would only take one shift of her hips to make me explode. But, I wanted a taste first.

I dropped to my knees and turned her so I was at eye level with her pretty pussy. "I've missed your honey, baby." A long, slow lick had her shuddering with need. I ate her pussy, savoring every bite, lick, and suck. I made her come twice before I was satisfied and surged to my feet, lifting her off the ground and impaling her as I pressed her against the wall.

"Oh fuck! You feel so good, baby."

She squeezed her inner muscles and I was on the verge of coming, so I began to pump into her, while I played with her clit. She was crying out and meeting my every thrust with her hips.

"You ready, baby? I'm going to come, Ellie! Fuck, I need you to come!"

Suddenly, she froze and I reared back in surprise.

"Condom, Jack," she panted.

I scowled. "Fuck the condom, Ellie. I only take you bare."

She mirrored my dark expression and opened her mouth to argue, but I didn't let her get a word out before covering her mouth with my own and driving in two more times, setting us both off.

After we had Addy, I'd agreed to wear a condom until Ellie was ready to try again, but the first time I tried it, I couldn't feel her and I pulled out, tore it off, and dove back inside. She was pretty pissed when she turned up pregnant three months later. I thought it was fucking fantastic and I told her so. She accused me of being a Neanderthal and stormed out of the room. With a little chocolate and a whole lot of eating her pussy, it didn't take me long to convince her to forgive me.

"Dad!" Addy yelled, banging on our bedroom door. "I know you're in there!"

I lifted my mouth from where I was devouring Ellie's honey and frowned. "Adult time, Addy!" I shouted, grateful I remembered to lock the door.

Ellie chortled and I glared at her.

"Why do I have to watch the other kids?" she whined.

"Because I said so. Now, go be a good daughter and give your mom and I some alone time."

She stomped away from the door, muttering loudly, "You better not be giving me another brother or sister!"

Ellie was all out laughing and I scowled. She held her hands up in a sign of surrender. "Hey, you're the one who decided five was the magic number."

The dark look on my face must have morphed into complete and utter shock because Ellie rolled her eyes and gave me a dry look.

"Five?" I croaked.

"Yup. What did you think would happen when you couldn't keep a rubber on your giant cock?"

I tried, I really did, but every time I felt something between us, I couldn't stand it. It was like I couldn't breathe until we were one.

After a moment the shock wore off and a smug smile crossed my face. I looked down at her currently flat stomach. *Way to go, boys.*

# Bonus Scene: A Puppy!

## Ellison

When Jack opened the front door and peeked his head inside with a mischievous look in his chocolate brown eyes, I should have known he was up to something. His dark hair was even more tousled than usual, and his tie looked like one of his patients had nibbled on it. If he'd had our youngest son with him, I would have understood the slobber on his tie. Ethan was twenty months old and his second set of molars were coming in, so he considered anything in the vicinity of his mouth fair game. But all the kids had been home with me today. All morning.

I was trying to get the house ready for Addy's tenth birthday party since we were about to be invaded by a swarm of her school friends. Jack had up and disappeared on me bright and early this morning. He'd claimed something urgent had come up at the hospital as he left me collapsed on our bed, boneless from the orgasm he'd given me. Before I'd been able to argue, he was gone.

Narrowing my eyes at him, I placed my hands on my hips and tried to give him the death glare. I felt myself quickly weakening, though, when he flashed me a boyish grin. "It's about time you made it back home. Addy's friends are going to be here any minute now."

"Sorry, baby." His tone was apologetic, but his expression hadn't changed at all, and he still hadn't stepped through the door. He was definitely up to something. "I didn't think it would take me this long, or I would have let you in on the surprise."

"Surprise?" I wasn't sure I liked the sound of that. Especially not on Addy's birthday, since our oldest girl had her daddy firmly wrapped around her finger. And then I heard it, a soft whining sound coming from behind Jack. He hadn't.

"A surprise, Daddy?" Addy gasped behind me, racing past me. "Please, please, please tell me it's what I hope it is!"

Before he pulled the little white ball of fluff from behind his back, I knew. He really had.

"A puppy!" she squealed. "This is the best birthday ever, Daddy!"

"Yes, Daddy. The best birthday ever," I agreed wryly. How could I really be upset when my baby girl was so happy? Although, it would have been nice if I'd known he was going to get her the puppy today. He'd just gotten me to agree to one this morning, right after he'd given me an orgasm.

Addy sat on the floor, her present crawling all over her. "Is it a boy or a girl puppy?"

"A boy," Jack answered, smiling down at our daughter before looking up at me. "A West Highland White Terrier. He's low shed, low dander, and built like a tank, so he can withstand the craziness of living with our five kids."

"Sounds like you put a lot of thought into this," I murmured, determined to give him a little bit of hell for this. Not too much, though, since he had gotten my okay before actually buying the puppy and bringing it home. "I'm amazed you were able to pick the perfect breed, find a litter of puppies, and select this one all this morning."

"Well, I might have had a little bit of a head start," he admitted sheepishly.

"Mmmhmm," I hummed.

"Do I get to name him?" Addy asked.

"Sure, baby girl."

"How about you pick two names and then Daddy and I will choose between them?" I added.

Her eyes turned mischievous, so much like her father's that my heart melted. "Okay, Mommy. We can name him Woofie or Martin."

*Woofie or Martin?* Yeah, my daughter knew how to get what she wanted. We went with Woofie. Obviously.

# Books By This Author

### Risqué Contracts Series

Penalty Clause

Contingency Plan

Fraternization Rule

### Yeah, Baby Series

Baby, You're Mine

Baby Steps

Baby, Come Back

# About the Author

Hello! My name is Fiona Davenport and I'm a smutoholic. I've been reading raunchy romance novels since... well, forever and a day ago it seems. And now I get to write sexy stories and share them with others who are like me and enjoy their books on the steamier side. Fiona Davenport is my super-secret alias, which is kind of awesome since I've always wanted one.

You can connect with me online on Facebook or Twitter.

Printed in Great Britain
by Amazon